LUKE LUDD

LUKE LUDD

•

D.J. Bishop

AVALON BOOKS
NEW YORK

Bis

PRINTED IN THE UNITED STATES OF AMERICA
ON ACID-FREE PAPER
BY HADDON CRAFTSMEN, BLOOMSBURG, PENNSYLVANIA

For
Guy G. Randall (Pop)

*My number one fan and whose faith in my story telling got me
started and kept me going.*

And to
Blanche Jamison

*Who, without her friendship and help in editing, this book
woud have never been published.*

And Let's Not Forget

*All the many true cowboys I've had the pleasure of knowing in
my life. May the ones still with us always be mounted fresh and
ride where the prairie is wide, the air clean, and the water
cool and clear. And to the many who have already rode over
the distant horizon and faded into the sunset, may they always
be remembered in a good light and wherever they are, may
they rest in peace.*

Grateful appreciation goes to:

Tommie, Virginia, Sam, Effie, Mary, Claude, Judy, Kelly, Jackie, Estelle, Donnie Joe, Joe Lee, Jay, L.W. (Jack) & Claudie May, Rocky and Denise because without their inspiration the story would have never been told; and a very special thanks to Major Guy G. Randall U.S.A.F.R.—retired and his lovely wife Lea for their undying faith and encouragement.

Chapter One

Knowing he had to stay conscious to stay alive, Luke Ludd dug his finger deep into the hole in his side. Pain tore through his body, opening his eyes to the dark realization that he was hurt—and hurt bad. He could not move his left arm or his right leg, and everywhere he touched, his body seemed to be covered in warm blood. He knew he had to move, that staying here—wherever he was—meant death, for they would surely find him. He had to find Mousy. He had left him saddled and tied somewhere, but with his mind distorted by the roaring pain in his body, he could not remember where. He did remember, and very clearly, the hot stabbing pain as the bullet tore into his left shoulder and again as another ripped at his side, and still another terrible pain washed over him as the third bullet entered his right leg just below the knee. He remembered falling, striking his face solidly against the hard-packed dirt street, and kicking and clawing at the hard ground trying to crawl and

1

ending up here. But where was here? Wherever here was, it was dark—so dark, in fact, he could barely see his hand passing in front of his face. He turned as best he could, looking back over his shoulder to see a dim light coming from somewhere. Working with his one good hand and leg, he gritted his teeth against the pain and pushed and pulled against the piers until he got turned to where he was facing in that direction. He peered out and was quick to realize he was under a boardwalk, but under what boardwalk? He wiped at his eyes with the back of his hand to clear the sweat and dirt; he looked again and after a moment of trying hard to focus his eyes, he made out a distant sign that read *General Store*. He knew then that he had to be due north of there, probably under the boardwalk somewhere near the barbershop.

The little town of Rising Star was quiet now; not a sound could be heard. The air hung heavy with the smell of burnt gunpowder, reminding him of what had just taken place. He let his eyes move slowly along the street. Dead bodies lay scattered here and there. Clint McKuen lay faceup on the boardwalk in front of the general store with a bullet hole between his eyes. Luke could not see the hole from his present position, but he knew its location because he had put it there just an instant before Clint pulled the trigger and sent the bullet flying that ripped into Luke's side.

Only a few feet away Clint's brother Robert, not yet twenty years old, was slumped headfirst in a water trough. And farther up the street in the entrance to the alley between the Driftwood Saloon and hotel, where the gunplay had started, lay still another one of the McKuen brothers— the one they called Porter.

With those three dead that just left Barton and Quint to deal with, but that was enough because Luke knew they were the worst of the lot. Of the five McKuen brothers those two were the smartest and the fastest with their guns, and both were known killers. Hearing footsteps coming along the boardwalk, he hunkered more closely to the ground, and as they come to a stop directly above him his pulse quickened.

"Have you seen anything?" a loud voice called out.

"No," a distant voice called back. "But he's got to be here somewhere, Barton. He's hit and hit hard. He's probably laying here dead somewhere and we just ain't found his body yet."

"That might be, Quint, but keep looking. Laughlin wants him dead and he wants him dead tonight. He told me, 'When you find 'im, if he's still alive, hang 'im in that big cottonwood down by the bridge; that way the whole town will be sure to see 'im.'" The voice paused, then added, "We'll find 'im. There's more men ridin' in from the ranch and they'll be here before long."

"More men!" Quint called out, his voice now getting closer. "Listen, Barton, we don't need more men to handle the likes of Luke Ludd."

"Look around, Quint. Do you see anyone but McKuens laying dead? Ludd's already killed three of us!"

"Yeah," Quint replied, "but if Porter would have done as he was told and shot 'im in the back, they'd all still be alive; he just wouldn't listen. I hate about old Clint being dead, but Porter and Robert—those two half-wits are probably better off."

"No need talking about it now," Barton said. "I'll go look in that old shack out behind the Driftwood and you go check the livery."

"Okay," Quint answered.

"If you see anything, let a shot go and I'll come running." Barton snorted, stepping from the boardwalk down to the street.

"You can count on that, big brother. I'll let one go all right, right between his eyes."

"Don't underestimate 'im, Quint. As long as Ludd's got a breath of air left in 'im he's dangerous, and if you don't watch your step he'll kill you too."

"Don't worry about me, Barton," Quint replied abruptly. "You just watch out for yourself."

Luke watched as Barton McKuen's thick body crossed the dirt street and made his way along the boardwalk. Luke lay still, not moving until the man had entered the alley and disappeared into its dark shadows. Thinking back on what had been said, he remembered where he had left Mousy. He had left him tied to that old cottonwood down by the bridge—the one they were planning to hang him in. But it was a good three, maybe four hundred yards from here to there, and he still hadn't figured out how he was going to get there without being seen.

Again, he felt consciousness slipping away, and he dug his finger deep into the hole, and the sudden sharp pain brought him back to life. He had heard them say, too, that more men were on their way. How many he did not know, but in his condition, he knew that any was too many.

He also realized that he could not crawl out the front, for along the street there would be no cover and they would surely see him. He must—if he went at all—crawl out the back to the creek and make his way along its banks under the cover of the trees and high grass. And he had to hurry because with each passing minute, he was growing weaker, and blood continued to pour freely from his wounds.

Reaching into his back pocket, he pulled out his handkerchief and placed it under his shirt over the wound in his shoulder. With that done, he took the bandanna from around his neck and put it over the gash in his side. Then taking his belt off, he used his one good hand and his teeth to tie it as best he could around his leg, hoping it would slow the flow of blood.

Reaching down for his gun, he felt nothing but leather. "Dang, I've lost it," he said under his breath. Moving his hand slowly along the ground, he found his old hat first, then the gun lying beside his leg. Feeling his hand against the gun barrel forced a short-lived smile to his lips. He flipped the cylinder open but in the darkness, he was unable to see how many, if any, bullets remained unspent. He dumped the contents of the cylinder out into his lap, then picking the cartridges up one at a time, he felt for a lead tip. The first two cartridges were spent and he dropped them to the ground. The next one had a lead point so he replaced it in the cylinder. The next three were also spent. Frantically, he felt along his gunbelt and found two more and added them to the pistol and closed the cylinder. Shoving the Colt down deep in the holster, he latched the leather thong over the hammer.

He turned toward the back of the building and started to crawl, working his way between the piers, but had only moved a few inches when he had to stop. He was too weak and the pain was too great. After a short rest, he blinked the sweat from his eyes and started on, but like the previous attempt, he did not get far before he had to stop. Again and again, he would crawl and stop. Once, he lost consciousness—for how long he did not know; he only knew that when he came to he didn't feel any better. With each attempt, he was getting closer—closer to the back wall, then it was another twenty yards or so from there to the outhouse, and another twenty or thirty yards beyond it to the creek, and all that way, he would be right out in the open, concealed by nothing but the darkness of night. Not until he reached the creek would there be any kind of cover. "Maybe I can find a stick, board, or something laying out back that I can use for a crutch," he said to himself. "But that would mean my right hand would be busy with it and make me a little slower on the draw—maybe too slow."

With that thought in mind he took a deep, ragged breath and crawled on. By the time he stopped again, he was within a few feet of the back wall, but he was tired, weak, and very sleepy. He had no more than came to a stop when he heard horse hooves pounding the hard ground as they made their way into town. From the sound Luke estimated there to be at least a dozen. He heard the loud voices of Barton and Quint McKuen greet the men as they drew up, and he knew then that time was running out.

He gritted his teeth against the pain and pushed on. Coming to the edge of the building, he paused again to catch his breath. Reaching down, he slipped the thong from over the hammer of the Colt and started crawling out from under the building. With his body no more than halfway clear, his head hit something that stopped him. He blinked his eyes to clear them, and there before him was an old pair of boots. He closed his eyes and relaxed, getting ready for the blast that would end his life, but then nothing.

He raised his head to see who was standing there, but in the darkness, he could not make out the face—all he could see was the muzzle of a double-barrel shotgun pointing straight at his head.

"Well, if you're going to shoot dammit—shoot, but it'll be a cold day in Hades before I beg," he said defiantly. But as he spoke the words the loss of blood and the weakness got the better of him and he dropped his head back to the ground. Then came the helpless, overwhelming feeling of unconsciousness, or maybe it was more—maybe it was the feeling of death.

Miles from town, a young woman walked from the little white house with a basket in her hand; she stepped from the porch headed in the direction of the chicken pen. She was a beautiful girl, tall and lean with a full head of long, thick, black hair that hung down in large curls almost to her hips. Her skin was soft and smooth, lightly tanned, and her eyes were big and dark. She was a happy girl, and it took very little to bring a smile to her lovely face.

She made her way across the yard to the water-well. There she stopped and set the basket on the edge of the well box. Hearing hogs squeal, she turned her attention northwest toward their pen and saw the reason for all the commotion. Her father had started toward them with a feed bucket in his hand. She watched as he fed old Sadie, the big black sow. Like every morning, the old gal was mad at the world and the hair was bristled along her back. As he poured the feed into her trough, the sow snapped viciously at the bucket.

Sadie was dangerous, and the girl knew it. She could not be turned out to graze with the rest of the hogs because she'd kill them, even though most of them were her own offspring. She was a good mother, but once the pigs were weaned she had no more use for them. Loraine had told her paw several times he needed to get rid of Sadie before she hurt him or someone else, but he rejected the idea and Loraine knew why. She knew that even though the old sow was mean, she had ten pigs to a litter, two times a year, and that kept plenty of pork in the smokehouse. And the

ones her paw sold in town meant money—money they depended on to live.

For Loraine Langtry this was the most beautiful time of
day. The sun was just now starting to peek over the oak-
covered hills to the east, and the fresh morning air was
damp and cool. She turned her dark brown eyes to the west
and let them move slowly along the hillside looking for
anything that didn't belong—anything that would give her
a clue that someone was watching her or the house. After
looking and listening she took up the basket and walked
on toward the chicken pen.

After gathering the eggs, she made her way back toward
the house, stopping just long enough at the barn to pick up
the bucket of milk that her paw had set there after milk-
ing the cow. With the bucket in one hand and the basket
of eggs in the other she crossed the yard and disappeared
into the little house.

Inside she set the eggs on the table and at the cabinet
she started straining the milk into a fresh pail. Hearing a
faint moan, she turned from her work and crossed the floor
to the door of the spare bedroom, pushed it open, and
stepped through. "Luke," she called out in a low voice.
"Are you awake?" Getting no response, she walked closer
and dropped to a chair beside the bed. Taking the rag from
his forehead, she rinsed it clean in a pan of cool water. And
after wringing it dry, she placed it back across his forehead.
"Oh, Luke, why did you have to come back?" she asked
while letting her fingers run slowly along his bearded face.
"They had already killed your paw and taken the ranch;
there was nothing you could do for 'im."

Lying before her, she did not see the hard-nosed railroad
agent with the fast gun that everyone talked about. She saw
only the square-jawed, brown-eyed boy who had grown up

on the next ranch over. The boy who had treated her all her life as a sister and who she considered to be the big brother she never had. What he'd done since leaving the ranch seven years ago she had no real knowledge of but she had heard he worked for the railroad—a Pinkerton Agent or something like that. His job was guarding gold shipments and tracking down robbers and such—people who had done wrong against the trains. "You're going to be all right," she said, reaching out and giving his hand a little pat. Slowly pushing up to her feet, she straightened her dress and went back to her chores.

She had just finished straining the milk and putting the eggs away when the door opened and the sight of her paw walking in brought a smile to her face.

"How's he doing?" Cork Langtry asked, dropping to a chair at the table.

"About the same," she replied, wiping her hands on her apron. "What are we going to do, Paw? It's been five days."

"Nothing much we can do, Loraine," he answered. After a short pause he said, "I reckon I could go into town and see if the doctor will come back out here again—I bet he won't. They almost caught 'im the last time coming back into town. Couldn't blame 'im if he said no. If they found out he'd been out here doctoring Luke, they'd kill 'im for sure."

"He needs some solid food," she commented. "That chicken broth and soup I've been force-feeding 'im is just barely keeping 'im alive."

"That's all he needs until he wakes up," the old man said. After pausing to think, he added, "You might see if you can get some of those raw eggs down 'im."

She gave her head a quick nod. "Yeah, now that might do 'im some good."

"I'm a-thinking Barton will be showing up around here any day now. I don't know why they haven't already been out here. I heard in town that they've made all the other ranches looking for 'im. They've got to know you two were close, and that old Luther and me were friends."

"I don't know why they haven't been out here either," she answered with a worried look on her face. "Paw, what are we going to do—when they do come?"

"We're going to act just like we always have, Loraine. I'll have no trouble with 'em unless they try to come in the house," the old man answered. Taking a deep breath, he let it out slowly, and said, "I wish your Uncle Elam would hurry up and get back from Caster."

"You know they'll want to come in and have a loo—," she started to say, but she suddenly stopped after hearing the sound of a loud groan coming from the bedroom. As she started in that direction, Cork stood up from the table and followed behind her. Stopping at the door, Loraine looked back at her father, she smiled and crossed her fingers on both hands for luck.

"Go on in, Loraine," Cork said. "Don't just stand out here grinning like a possum in a fig tree."

Slowly she pushed the door open and walked in. "Luke, are you awake?" she asked, but like before she got no response.

Her paw standing behind her nudged her forward, moving her deeper into the room. Stepping around her, he walked to the side of the bed. "Luke," he called out in a loud voice. "Can you hear me, son?" The man lying there did not move and made no sound. "Luke," Cork called out again, but still nothing. He dropped to the chair. Reaching, he took the injured man by the hand. "Luke, can you hear me?" he asked again, but this time, he had no more than got the words out of his mouth when he felt it—a light squeeze on his hand. He quickly turned to his daughter and said, "He hears me, Loraine; he just squeezed my hand."

"Move, Paw, get out of the way," she said, hurriedly pushing her way between the chair and bed. Reaching, she took Luke's hand and as she did, he lightly squeezed again and the light pressure brought a smile to her lips and a tear of joy to her eye. "He's going to be all right, Paw. Thank heaven, he's going to be okay."

"Well," the old man mumbled, letting out a long, hard, ragged breath. "Now that he's coming around, we need to find somewhere we can hide 'im. Somewhere he'll be safe from Barton and that bunch." He stood up from the chair and said, "Loraine, I'll be out in the barn if you need me."

"Okay, Paw."

Cork walked from the room. After sitting a bit longer, Loraine went back to her chores, but every so often she'd open the door and look in to see if Luke's eyes were open.

Out in the barn, Cork worked the rest of the day, pounding and sawing, and Loraine did not see him again until supper. "What have you been doing out there all day, Paw? I've been hearing all the hammering and sawing you've been doing."

"I've got an idea, girl," he answered. "Out in the barn, I've built a hay-manger in one of the stalls. After dark we're going to move Luke into it and cover 'im with hay. Then I'm going to put Sadie in there with 'im—I want to see Barton or anyone else for that matter try to go in there with her."

Loraine looked over at her paw, puzzled over his comment, and asked. "What's going to keep Sadie from getting Luke?"

"I've got all of that worked out," he answered. "All

we've got to worry about is getting that old hog from her pen to the barn without losing an arm or a leg."

"I don't know, Paw. That's going to be awful risky."

"What's risky, girl, is Luke laying there in that bedroom and a-thinkin' that Barton and that bunch won't find 'im. Now let's eat our supper; it'll be dark before long."

It was well after midnight when the old man walked out onto the porch. He stood, letting his eyes scan the hillside both east and west, looking and listening for anything—a flicker from a campfire or a snort from a horse. When satisfied that all was clear, he turned and walked back into the house. "Let's go, Loraine," he said. Taking a chair from the table, he started toward the bedroom. "We've got to be careful with 'im. We don't want to open 'im up and get 'im to bleeding again." He set the chair beside the bed; throwing the covers back, he eased Luke's unconscious body from the bed and set him in the chair. Leaning it back on two legs, he said, "Now back up to those chair legs, Loraine, and pick it up—this is the only way we can move 'im with his leg being shot up the way it is."

The girl did as she was told and after carrying Luke to the barn they placed the chair gently on the ground. The old man stepped quickly to the ladder and made his way up it to the loft where he threw down some hay. "Loraine," he called down in a low voice. "Put enough of that hay in the bottom of the manger to make it soft; then we'll put Luke in on top of it."

Loraine did as instructed, and as she did, she noticed what a fine job her paw had done in building it. He had built a manger all right, but on the inside, he had made a box and it was in that box that Luke would be placed. After putting down a nice thick layer of hay for the injured man to lie on, they lifted him over the side and down into the box. Making sure they left a gap between the boards, so he could get air, they placed them over the top and nailed them down, covering the boards with more hay.

Now came the hard part, getting old Sadie from her pen into the stall. The old man turned. "You wait here," he said, walking from the barn. He was not long in returning with a squealing pig in each hand and placed them in the next stall. Tying a rope to the gate leading into the stall that Luke was in, he handed the other end to Loraine and said, "Give me enough time to get back to the pens, then I want you to get those pigs to squealing. Pull their tails and ears, whatever you have to do, but we need 'em to be making plenty of noise. I'll let old Sadie out and she should come running. When she goes into that stall there, you pull the rope and close the gate."

"Okay, Paw," Loraine replied. "You be careful."

The night was pitch black. No moon was shining and very few stars could be seen. Cork made his way through the darkness to the pen where Sadie met him with her usual onslaught of defiant grunts. The old man stopped at the gate and waited for the pigs to start squealing, and as they did the old black sow went into a fit of violent anger. After he was sure that she was really worked up, he slung open the gate. Instantly the old hog ran at him with her mouth open, but as she did, he jumped over the fence to safety and she ran on toward the barn and the sound of the squealing pigs.

Loraine heard her coming and as she got closer the girl's pulse quickened, but she had not realized just how frightened she really was until the huge mass of black muscle came through the door and got within the glare of the flickering lantern. Without stopping she ran past the open gate that led into the stall that Luke was in and stuck her long, black snout between the rails of the stall where Loraine knelt with the pigs. She grunted and snorted, sniffing hard at the air trying to figure out what was making the pigs squeal, but after getting the scent of Loraine's presence, she bristled her hair. At that moment the old man slammed one of the big doors leading into the barn shut. Sadie turned and ran as fast as she could tying to get out before the other door was closed, but before she got there, the old man slammed it closed, blocking her escape. She turned back toward the stalls, and as she came to the open gate, she walked in and when she did Loraine pulled hard on the rope closing the gate. "We've got her, Paw," the girl's shaky voice called out.

The old man opened the door just enough for him to squeeze through; then closing it behind him as he entered, he ran to the stall and latched the gate. He mopped the cold, nervous sweat from his forehead with a sleeve, then turning to Loraine, he smiled and said, "You did good."

"Paw, now we've got her in there, how am I going to look after Luke? I can't go in there with her."

"I'll open the gate to both stalls and when she comes out of this one I'll try to drive her into the other from the loft up there. You can take care of Luke, then we'll put her back. I just hope Luke don't go to bleeding or making a lot of noise or she'll have a fit trying to get to 'im." Cork fed the hog some grain and after blowing out the lantern, they made their way to the house and went to bed.

The next morning, he moved the remaining eight of Sadie's pigs into the stall with the other two and when he opened the gate to the stall that she was in, she came out and went straight into the next stall and lay down to let her pigs suck. Loraine fed and took care of Luke. And again that evening they did it all over again. By the end of the third day the old hog was making the change from one stall to the other without much trouble, even acting as though she didn't really mind.

That night after supper the old man sat on the porch in the cool night air having a smoke and sipping a cup of coffee. Looking west, he noticed something about halfway up the hill, a flicker from a campfire or something. He stood, looking more closely, but did not see it again. Turning, he walked slowly into the house. "They're watching us," he said.

"Who's watching?" Loraine asked.

"Barton and that bunch of no-goods, I reckon. I saw a flicker from a campfire. They're the only ones I know that would be camped out watching the house." Cork took a deep, worried breath. "I should have left 'im in town, Loraine. We can't hold off that whole bunch by ourselves— they'll kill me, and after they do no telling what to you, they'll kill you too."

"Paw, you did the right thing; you couldn't just leave Luke there. They would have killed 'im for sure."

"Oh, you're right, Loraine," he answered. "I don't know what I get to thinking sometimes. Well, anyway, it's done and we can't change it now. We've been dealt the cards; now we'll just have to wait and see if anybody raises the bet." Pushing up from the table, he said, "I think I'll go to bed, Loraine. Good night."

"Good night, Paw," she replied.

After washing and drying the last plate from supper, she put it in the cupboard. Untying her apron, she hung it on a peg by the door and made her way across the floor to her own bedroom where she was not long in getting in bed.

A rooster crowing the next morning marked the start of a new day. After gathering the eggs, Loraine stopped at the barn and took up the pail of milk. As she made her way across the yard, she turned her attention toward the south and the sound of horse hooves pounding the hard ground. Her face whitened at the sight of Barton McKuen as he led a group of five men from the lane into the yard.

"Mornin', Miss Loraine," he said, reining in his horse. "We need to talk to your paw. Is Cork here?"

"Yes, he is," she answered. "What do you need to talk to Paw about?"

"That's okay, Loraine," Cork called out, walking from the barn with his shotgun lying easy in the hollow of his arm. "What can I do for you fellows?" he asked.

Barton turned in the saddle, and at the sight of the shotgun, he quickly dropped his hand for the butt on his six-gun.

"I wouldn't do that if I was you, Barton," Cork said quickly, thumbing back both hammers. "From where I stand I don't think you'd have much of a chance."

"Oh, heck, Cork, you don't have to do that. We're not looking for trouble with you or the girl here. We're looking for that Luke Ludd. You know 'im, Cork; he grew up on the place just southwest of here."

"Yeah, I know Luke all right—knew his old pappy too. But I ain't seen nothing of that boy since he lit a shuck from these parts, I guess nigh seven years ago."

"I know you know 'im," Barton snorted. "And I think you know where he's at. You'd be saving yourself and your girl here a lot of trouble if you'd just tell us."

The old man's eyes narrowed. "Told you, Barton. I don't know where he's at, but if I did know, I wouldn't tell you."

"Would you mind if we took a look around? If he ain't here you've got nothing to worry about."

"If you want to take a look, go ahead, Barton, but just

you and Quint. I don't know these other men, so they can stay in their saddles."

"Well, that's fair enough, Cork," Barton replied, stepping to the ground. Turning, he handed his reins up to a man with a stone-cold face and wearing two six-guns. Then he and Quint walked into the house. It wasn't long before they came out, and walked from the porch in the direction of the barn. "What have you got in there?" Barton asked.

"Just my horses, an old milk cow, and a sow with a litter."

"Hogs?" Quint demanded. "What's wrong with keeping 'em out there in the pen with the rest?"

"She's sick," Cork replied, shaking his head worriedly. "Got hold of some locoweed or something. So if you go in there you better watch her."

The two men swung open the doors and walked in and as they made their way along the hall they took a good, long look in all the stalls. Coming to the stall where Sadie was, they stopped. She ran at the gate snorting, popping her teeth together hard like a mad dog. They jumped back quickly, drawing their guns. "I ain't never seen anything like that," Barton said. He nodded his head toward the old wooden ladder and said to his brother, "Go on up and have a look."

Quint, with his gun drawn, made his way slow and easy up the ladder, taking one rung at a time. Reaching the top, he stepped onto the floor of the loft, and started his search, but after a long, intense look, he called down, "Ain't nothing up here but hay." And with that said, he returned to the bottom where the two men, satisfied the man they sought was nowhere to be found, walked out.

"Don't you think you should have a closer look in that stall where that old hog is?" Cork asked.

"You must be out of your mind, Cork," Barton yelped. "That old sow will eat a man alive and you know it." He shook his head. "No, if Ludd was in there . . . there would be body parts scattered about." He glanced at Quint, then back at Cork. "No, sir, I'll just take your word that he's not in there. He'd stand a better chance out here with us than he would in there with that old crazy thing." The two men walked slowly from the barn to the horses and after taking up his reins, Barton turned and said, "I know if you did happen to see 'im you'd let me or Mr. Laughlin know, wouldn't you, Cork? There might be a reward in it for you, but even if there's not, you'd be doing right to tell us. If nothing else it would save you and your girl a lot of trouble."

"I'm not worried about any trouble you might try to give me, Barton," Cork said with a grin. "I've dealt with men like you before."

Barton's eyes narrowed. "Don't push your luck, old man. I've let you get by with throwing down on us with that shotgun. But if I was you I'd not do that again. If you do, I'll kill you." Swinging into leather, Barton McKuen turned his horse and led the group along the trail south.

Loraine walked to where her paw stood watching the men ride away, and as she approached, he said, "We've not seen the last of that bunch, Loraine. No, sir, we sure haven't. And I can tell Luke one thing—and that is, he's in trouble. Big trouble. Not from Barton or Quint; heck, he can handle them, but from those other four men. Two of 'em I recognized. The big one—the one wearing the black suit and flat-brimmed hat—is Roscoe Nash. And the other one—the one with the drooping red mustache, and wearing the white shirt and black vest—is Bill Powers, both top-notched gunfighters. I saw some of their handiwork one time over in Caster. Both of 'em faster than rattlesnakes with their guns, and twice as deadly."

"Who were the other two, I wonder, Paw?" Loraine asked.

"I don't know for sure, but if I had to guess I'd say two men of about the same background. Laughlin has hired 'im some top-hand gunslingers this time. He must really want Luke dead." He turned to face Loraine. "We better watch what we do for the next few days, girl, 'cause they'll be watching us. Let's try not to make so many trips out to the barn during the day. We don't want 'em gettin' any more suspicious than they already are."

"Okay," she replied.

"Frank Clancy and Heath Benson," a voice called out from behind them.

Startled by the loud voice, they turned to see a man dressed in a buckskin shirt and pants walking from behind the barn.

"Uncle Elam, you're back!" Loraine said happily.

"Who are Frank Clancy and Heath Benson?" Cork asked his brother.

"The other two men—the skinny one, with the freshly shaved face, and wearin' the black vest and striped shirt— is Frank Clancy. And the one wearing the two six-guns tried to his legs and the long, red droopin' mustache—I don't know for sure but I think that's Heath Benson. I don't know who they're after, but whoever it is, I can tell 'em for a fact—they're in for a rough ride."

"It's Luke Ludd, Uncle Elam," Loraine replied. "That's who they're after."

"Luke," Elam echoed, shaking his head. "I knew he'd show up. I don't know 'im, but after what you two have told me about 'im, I figured when he heard his paw had been shot dead he'd come back. Where's he at?"

"Out in the barn," Cork answered, turning toward the house. "Come on in and I'll tell you about it. It all started the day after you left for Caster."

In the house the two men sat at the table; Elam nodded a thank-you to Loraine as she sat a cup of hot coffee down on the table in front of him. Picking it up, he gave it a short, cooling blow, then a taste. "What's the story about Luke?" he asked, looking over the rim of the cup in his brother's direction.

"Before we get into that," Cork said, "what did you find out over in Caster?"

"I found out that Laughlin has taken over three ranches in the last two months. Arnett sold out to 'im first. Then he bought the Redwine place," he said, looking up from his coffee. "He just gave twenty cents an acre for that place. Then, of course, he got the Ludd place after they found old Luther shot dead. The only one he hasn't got is this one, Cork, and it's right in the middle."

"Twenty cents an acre is what he offered me for this place. That was for cattle and all," Cork replied in a low voice. "I told 'im to get off my property and don't come back."

"What about this deal with Luke?" Elam asked.

"Luke's in bad shape, he's all shot up, but he killed three of those sorry McKuen brothers. He's got a hole in his arm, another in the gut, and still another in his leg. The doctor came out and patched 'im up, but he hasn't woke up yet. I don't know if he's going to make it or not." The old man threw up a hand toward the west. "He's out there in the barn; that's the only place I could think of to hide 'im. Got 'im bedded down in a hay-manger out there."

"In the barn?" Elam half shouted. "That's a crazy place to keep a man with holes in 'im." He quickly stood up from the table.

"What are you going to do?" Cork asked.

"The first thing we're going to do is get that man out of the barn and back in the house here so Loraine can look after 'im. Then we'll have to take care of the other as it comes."

The two men left the house and in no time returned with Luke. After putting him back in bed, Loraine went right to work changing his bandages. She had not known her Uncle Elam long—she had heard about him all her life, but had never seen him until five years ago when her mother passed away. Shortly after her death, he showed up and had been hanging around ever since. She knew, from what her paw had told her, that his brother had lived a hard life. Most of it was spent fighting Indians and scouting for the Cavalry up north. And she had learned since his coming to the ranch that he didn't like being inside and preferred sleeping up in the hills on the ground. And he had made it very clear that he liked his coffee strong. "How can any two men be so much alike, but yet be so different," she muttered in a low voice to herself. From a distance she could hardly tell them apart. Their stature was about the same; both were tall, lanky, rawboned men, with lean bodies and sloping shoulders. Even though her Uncle Elam's hair was thinner and a bit longer, it was the same silver-gray color as her paw's. Their faces too were a whole lot alike, thin and stern, leathered brown by the hot sun, and the deep lines on both showed men up in their years. They even had the same steel-gray eyes. The only real difference Loraine could see between the two men was in their nature. Her paw was a loving man, easygoing—a man willing to listen to what a person had to say, but still not a man that could be pushed around. But her Uncle Elam was harsh, straightforward and to the point, a man who earned the respect of the people around him with his fist and gun, a man who once he got his mind set to doing something, seemed to be hell-bent on seeing it got done.

After she had finished changing Luke's bandages, she adjusted the pillow under his head, and pulled the cover up over his body; picking up the pan of water from the little table beside the bed, she turned and walked toward the door. Just as she reached for the handle, she heard her Uncle Elam say, "Laughlin's already took over everything around you, Cork. But he's got to have your place to make it all come together, and when he gets his hands on it he'll have control of all the water in this valley. Oh, they'll be coming all right; you can count on that. And when they do, they'll have blood in their eyes. It will either be kill or be killed."

Chapter Two

It had been two long, worrisome days since Barton and his bunch of killers had paid their little visit to the ranch, and Luke had been moved back into the house. He still had not opened his eyes, but for the past couple of days, his moans had been coming more regular and as the days passed they were getting louder, bringing him closer to consciousness.

Loraine added wood to the stove and put a piece of fatback in the pot of beans she was cooking for supper. Hearing a loud groan, she wiped her hands on the front of her apron and crossed to the bedroom door. She pushed it open and stuck her head in, and her eyes filled with surprise when she saw his head move. "Luke!" she called out. "Are you awake?" Then she saw his hand jerk a little. She crossed to the side of the bed. Reaching down, she removed the rag from his forehead and as she did his eyes opened.

She lifted her smiling face toward the heavens and said in a loud voice, "Thank you, Lord."

"Loraine," he said in a weak voice. "What are you doing here? Where am I? How long have I been here?"

"The answer to your first question is, I live here. The second is, you are at my house and the answer to your third question, Luke, is ten days. You want to know anything else?"

With his right hand, Luke lazily rubbed at the growth of whiskers along his jaw. All of a sudden his face twisted and he grabbed at the stabbing pain growing from his left shoulder. "Oh, that hurts," he said through gritted teeth. Looking up, he asked, "What happened to me, Loraine?"

"You almost got your fool self killed, that's what happened," she answered. "You got in a gunfight with those McKuen brothers. Paw said you killed three of 'em, but in getting that done they shot you up pretty bad. You've got one hole in your left shoulder, one in the side, and another one in you're right leg. You're lucky to be alive, Luke. Paw found you crawling out from under the barbershop and brought you here. That was ten days ago."

"I remember now," he said. After a short pause, he asked, "Where's Mousy?"

"Don't you worry none about him. Paw's got 'im staked out in that big grove of pecan trees east of here. You remember, Luke—down by the creek where you and me used to go riding all the time."

"You've got to get me out of here, Loraine," he moaned. "They'll be coming after me and there's no need in you and your family getting tangled up in all this mess."

"They were here two days ago," she replied bitterly. "Barton, Quint, and four other men. Paw knew two of 'em; he said their names was Roscoe Nash and Bill Powers. And my Uncle Elam recognized the other two as being Frank Clancy and Heath Benson. But they didn't find you 'cause me and Paw had you bedded down out in the barn in a hay-manger with old Sadie."

"Sadie?" he questioned. "Who's Sadie?"

"Oh," the girl replied blushingly. "Not a girl, but a hog. I'll tell you about her later. Right now you need to rest. You hungry? You want to try to eat something?"

He nodded his head. "I bet a plate of those beans I smell cooking would be awful good."

"It'll be a while before they're ready, Luke, but I've got some stew in there left over from supper last night."

"That'll be fine, Loraine," he said with an easy nod. "A man's got to start somewhere."

Loraine smiled, then turning from the bed she said, "I'll be right back." But by the time she returned, he had drifted back into a deep sleep. She set the plate down on the little table by the bed and dropped to the chair. For a long moment she sat staring hopelessly into the thin, pale face of the man who lay there. Reaching, she took his hand and brought it up, letting it slowly caress her soft face, and at the end of the short journey, she gave his hand a little kiss. For as long as she could remember, she had loved Luke Ludd, not as a sister loves a brother like most folks thought, but as a woman would love a man. For years she had kept her feelings to herself, horrified by the thought of what he might say, or worse yet, what he might think of her. But she lived each day in hopes that sooner or later he might realize how she felt and figure out that he felt the same way about her. But when he left seven years ago, she knew then that he could not possibly feel the same way about her because if he had, he would have never left. And when he didn't return within the first year, she was not sure herself

if she still felt the same way about him. But all the doubt
had disappeared the moment her paw brought him home.

With a shaky hand, she wiped the tears from her eyes,
and slowly pushed up from the chair and made her way
back to the kitchen where she added water to the pot of
boiling beans. Reaching, she raised the lid to the Dutch
oven and the room filled with the pleasant aroma of the
cooking cornbread. Hearing horses coming up the lane, she
crossed to the window, pushed back the curtains, and
looked out to see her paw and her Uncle Elam drawing up
at the hitch rail in front of the barn.

Crossing to the door, she walked out onto the porch and
stood with her hands on her hips, smiling big as the two
men made their way along the walk. As they approached
the steps, she said in a quiet voice, "Luke came to."

Her paw, leading the way, jerked his head at the news
and asked, "Did he say anything?"

"Yeah, he asked where he was, and how long he'd been
here. I told 'im I was going to get 'im something to eat,
but when I got back with the plate of stew, he had already
dozed off again."

"Here," Elam said, taking a bottle from his pocket.
"While we were in town we stopped by the doc's office
and picked up this here bottle of laudanum in case Luke's
going to need it, what with all his wounds."

"Oh, thank you, Uncle Elam. I'm glad you did because
we were almost out." But thinking about what he had said,
Loraine turned, quickly letting her eyes scan along the
south trail. "You didn't let anyone see you at his office,
did you?"

"Well, he didn't really give it to us," Elam confessed.
"We had seen 'im down at the café and told 'im in a quiet
way what we needed. It just so happened when we got to

his office and turned into the alley I looked through an open window and saw it sitting on his desk. I reached my hand in and got it."

"Did you see anything of Laughlin or his men?"

"The whole town's crawling thick with 'em," her paw interrupted. Shaking his head, he added, "They're everywhere you look—Laughlin's planning something big, but I can't figure out what, and we couldn't get anyone in town to talk. Looks to me like the whole town is scared to death."

"They've got every right to be," Elam cut in. "You put that many fast guns in one town and sooner or later somebody's going to get killed. Each one's just waitin' for someone to make a mistake so they can prove to the others how fast they are."

Cork stepped to the porch, looking back to his brother. "Wonder why Laughlin ain't made his move on this place?"

"I don't know," Elam replied. "I've been wondering the same thing. He will—I know it and you do too. We've got to be ready, Cork; we can't let 'em slip up on us like they did old Luther. We've got to keep our eyes open to everything around us."

Loraine led the way into the house. At the table the two men dropped to chairs while she poured each a hot cup of coffee. "What could it be, Paw?" she asked. "I'm awful worried. What could Laughlin and his bunch be up to?"

"I wish I had an answer, Loraine, but I don't. It seems to me to be more than just the land and water. If that was what he wanted, all he'd have to do is send them hired guns of his out here to kill us off like he did Luke's paw."

"That's all he wants," a weak voice called out.

The sudden words sent both men, sitting at the table, instantly to the floor grabbing for their guns.

"Luke!" Loraine yelled. "What are you doing out of bed?"

"Heard voices," he replied. "Thought I'd come see what all the commotion was about."

She crossed to where he weakly stood propped against the door, and taking him by the arm, she helped steady him. "You get yourself right back in there, Luke Ludd." Turning back, she called out, "Paw, Uncle Elam, come help me quick!"

As the two men approached where the injured man stood, Luke's legs buckled and he started to fall, but with Loraine holding to his arm, he stayed up long enough for Cork and Elam to reach out and grab him. With a man on each side, they got him back to the bed and as they lowered him onto its side, the consciousness he had so briefly known slipped away.

Loraine grabbed the bottle of laudanum sitting on the nearby table and after pouring a spoon level full, she opened his mouth with her fingers and poured it in. "He'll sleep now."

"That man's got some grit," Elam commented. "No wonder he gave them McKuens such a hard time." He looked down into the face of the man lying there, and mumbled, "Wonder what he knows?" Glancing back to his brother, he added, "He said the land and water is all Laughlin's after."

Loraine adjusted the pillow under Luke's head and pulled the covers up over his body. Turning from the bed, the three walked back to the kitchen.

Later after having his fill of beans and cornbread, Elam slid back his chair and stood up. "I reckon I'll light a shuck," he said with a laugh. "Got to get my beauty sleep.

Loraine, that was sure some mighty fine grub. You make a man proud to call you his niece."

"Why, thank you, Uncle Elam," she said with a bashful giggle.

Cork raised slowly from his chair. "I wish you'd think about maybe beddin' down here in the house with us."

"Couldn't get no rest, Cork. I don't see how anyone gets any sleep all cooped up. No, I'll just mosey along, but don't worry, I'll be close by." He paused to think, then asked, "Loraine, have you maybe got an empty flour sack or something over there you can load a few supplies in for me?"

"Yes, I do, Uncle Elam. I've got a couple of clean flour sacks," she answered. "Where are you going?"

"I want you to load one with a few cans of beans and maybe a piece or two of that cornbread there that we had left over and a little bacon if you've got a-plenty."

"Where are you going, Uncle Elam?" Loraine asked again.

"You don't worry yourself about where I'm going, girl. You just get the sack loaded."

While Loraine loaded the beans and bread, her paw walked from the house in the direction of the smokehouse and returned with a side of bacon, and after adding it to the sack Elam took it and started out. At the hitch rail, he hung the sack over the pommel. Stepping around the horse, he slid the Winchester from its boot and checked it, making sure it had a full load. With that done, he pulled at the cinch and stepped into leather. Swinging the zebra dun north, he rode from the yard and as he made his way across the hard-packed ground, he threw up a good-bye hand to his brother and niece who stood on the porch watching him go.

He wanted it to appear to anyone watching that he was

pulling up stakes, dragging out, leaving only his brother and niece at the ranch. He knew that staying together meant death for all, that Barton and his bunch when given the order would swoop down on the ranch from the hills and kill everything in their way. Everyone would have to die and Elam knew it, for Laughlin could not afford to leave witnesses to any such massacre—someone who might go to the sheriff and tell of his evil deed, thus spoiling his plans to take control of the water that in turn would give him full control over the valley, the town, and the people in it.

Elam rode on north. Coming to the north fork of Dead Cow Creek, he drew up and let the dun have his head to drink. He turned his eyes to the ground looking for a sign, but saw nothing that had been made by man. Turning an ear to the wind, he listened for sound and heard only a soft trickle from the water as it made its way among the rocks, and from the distant west the yelp of a lonely coyote. "From day one it's been all about control," he mumbled to himself. Thinking back to when Maxwell Laughlin first come to Rising Star, just a mere three years ago, he could see it clearly now. Within the first week, he had opened his own bank and before the month was out, he had bought out the general store and both saloons.

The Driftwood was the first saloon Laughlin took control of and where he now had his office set up in the back room. And next was the Ann Mayre just a few doors down. The second year, he purchased the dry goods store, and later that same year the livery stable, but the higher prices he was charging and the much higher interest at the bank brought angry criticism from the town folks, and to get them off his back, he had a church built. Shortly after the completion of it, he attended a town meeting where he proposed the name of the town be changed from Rising Star to Maxwell. The town folks immediately put it to a vote and the idea was unanimously voted down. After hearing the outcome, he jumped up from his chair and stormed from the meeting, cursing at the people as he passed, and shortly after that he started buying up land.

Hearing a crow squawk, Elam jerked his head in that direction, but after giving the area a long, hard look and seeing nothing out of the ordinary, he touched the dun with a spur and crossed the creek. Turning at right angle, he swung the horse back south toward the ranchhouse. Keeping to thick cover, he worked his way along, stopping from time to time to check his back trail. He had not seen anything that gave him the slightest clue that someone was following, but he had an awful feeling deep in his gut, and over the years he had learned to trust and depend on just such feelings to keep him alive.

Of the four men who rode with the two McKuen brothers that day at the ranch, Elam knew none personally, but at one time or another he had heard of them all. Roscoe Nash was a half-breed—his father a Scottish cattle buyer, his mother a Pawnee squaw. He was a man who tracked with his mind as well as his senses. And while his eyes searched out the meaning of a trail, his mind would be looking far ahead trying to determine the direction and destination of the man he trailed. Elam had heard that Roscoe was as smart as they come and could track a feather across a solid bed of rock. But he would not be the one doing the following now nor would it be Heath Benson, Frank Clancy, or Bill Powers. It would be none of them, for they would be in town staying close to Laughlin, awaiting his orders. No, if someone was riding his back trail it would be one of the lesser men, maybe Barton or Quint or maybe both.

He turned his eyes toward the western horizon where the sun hung low and its reddish-orange glare streaked the far-off sky, sending the shadows of the mighty oak long and jagged to the east, casting a dark-gray haze over the valley. He rode on south, picking his way through the trees; getting within sight of the ranchhouse, he continued on until he came upon a outcropping of boulders. From among them he would have a good view of the trail leading south into town, and also the ranchhouse, and here his campfire would be concealed from the searching eyes of others.

He swung down and after stripping the saddle from the dun, he led him to a little knoll of good grass and put the hobbles on. On his way back, he gathered limbs from a nearby dead-fall and built a small fire. After adding water to the coffeepot, he set it over the flames.

It was dark now; neither house below nor anything around it could be made out, but the glare of the light coming from the windows told him that his brother and niece were still getting about. Loraine was probably working in the kitchen doing something like cleaning or such, and Cork by this time was sitting in front of the fire reading the Good Book, like he had done every night since his beloved Estelle had passed.

In the corral just south of the barn the horses mingled, and even though Elam could not see them he could hear them snort from time to time, clearing their nostrils of dust.

He dropped to the ground by the fire and after the coffee had cooked, he poured a cup; then bringing it up he gave it a cooling blow and tasted it. "Now that's the way to make coffee," he said under his breath. To the west a coyote cried to the moon and to the north another answered him, and in a nearby tree an owl hooted and took wing, and in another a nightingale whistled a mating call. The wind blew light from the west, bringing life to the leaves high in the trees above, and they danced to the rhythm of the cool night air.

The sounds he heard were all too familiar; he had spent his whole life, or a good bit of it, listening and learning, and he had stayed alive knowing what sounds belonged where and when and what sounds didn't. And too, he saw things differently than most people—he could look at a track made by man, beast, or fowl and not only know what had made it but why it was there in the first place, and he had many a time saved his own bacon by following the tracks of an unseen creature to a seep of water coming up under a rock or in the trunk of an old tree. But of all he had learned, patience was the hardest. Sitting in one place for days on end waiting and watching for an Indian brave or squaw to make their move, and when they did, he followed them straight to a camp the Cavalry had spent months searching for. And knowing when to stand and fight and when to light a shuck was something else that had over the years saved his hair a time or two.

He glanced back to the house, and now the windows were dark. He flipped the last few drops of coffee from the cup and pushed up from the ground. Standing, he stretched his arms high over his head and gave a tired groan. Then letting his eyes scan the camp, he picked the spot most likely for his bedroll, and after putting it down, he placed rocks along its length and covered them with a blanket. He put his saddle at the end where his head should be and placed his hat down as though it was covering his eyes. Turning from there, he walked to where he had left the mustang hobbled. Leading him back to camp, he tied him to a nearby tree, knowing that if anyone should try to approach while he was asleep the horse would be the first to know. Taking up his Winchester, he crossed to a giant old oak and dropped to the ground beside it. He slowly let his eyes search the hillside both near and far, looking and listening, and as the flames from his own campfire flickered for the last time, he slowly closed his eyes.

It was still dark when his eyes opened to the sound of dry leaves rustling somewhere to his not-too-distant left. He cut a quick eye to the mustang that stood with his head high and ears perked looking in the direction from which the sound had come. Letting his fingers move slowly, he tightened his grip on the stock of the Winchester lying across his lap. Keeping his head still, he let his eyes slowly move in that direction further and further until he saw what was making the noise. An armadillo was digging around the base of one of those rocks in search of grubs. A worried, somewhat aggravated sigh fell from Elam's lips, then a flash of anger washed over him as he wondered how anything had gotten so close without him hearing it. "I'm gettin' too old," he mumbled to himself. He sat for a moment longer listening and watching, and when satisfied that all sound and movement had been identified, he stood up and at the still-smoldering embers, he added kindling. Dropping down to one knee, he blew at the ashes and moments later a light wisp of smoke rose, then a flicker of flame. He moved the coffeepot near the growing flames, then standing he led the dun to the little knoll to graze. Back at the campfire, he sliced bacon into a pan and by the time it had fried the sun was coming up and night was giving way to the dim, hazy light of day.

He ate as he watched his brother walk from the house. At the corral, Cork pitched hay to the horses; then he disappeared into the barn, but a short time later, he reappeared and set a bucket down by the door. From there, he made his way with a feed bucket in hand toward the hogpen.

A sudden movement caught Elam's eye, and he turned his attention back to the yard just in time to see Loraine crossing to the chicken pen with her basket. After gathering the eggs and throwing the chickens a little grain, she took up the milk pail and went back to the house.

From where he sat it seemed to be just the start of another beautiful day, but in the pit of his stomach, he still had that awful feeling—the feeling that something was going to happen, the feeling that things were just not right. He let his eyes move back over the hillside; then standing, he kicked dirt on the fire. Its flames quickly dwindled, leaving behind only a few puffs of light, blue-gray smoke.

He made his way to where the dun was grazing, and after leading him back to camp, he saddled him, loaded the coffeepot and skillet into the saddlebags, and hung the sack of supplies over the pommel. He scooped out a hole in the earth and buried the remains of the campfire, and after filling the hole, he placed a flat rock over the top to conceal the freshly dug dirt. Breaking a limb from down low on a nearby scrub cedar, he swept out his tracks as best he could. He knew that a seasoned tracker like Nash would not be fooled by any such attempt to cover a trail, but it might slow Barton or someone else that might be following. Stepping into leather, he swung the dun south and rode slow among the oak. He rode with his ears keen to the sounds around him and his eyes cast toward the ground looking for a track or a broken twig or the remains of a campfire— anything that might give him a clue as to what Laughlin's men were up to, but more important how many. He rode on but always within sight of the house, for he knew that the attack could come at any moment and he had to be ready—ready to ride in from an unsuspected direction and take the would-be killers by surprise.

Back at the house Loraine had finished straining the milk, and was standing at the cabinet washing the eggs, when an uneasy feeling swept over her. Reaching, she pushed back the curtains and looked out to see her father making his way toward the barn from the hogpen. Hearing a shuffling noise behind her, she spun.

"Thought I might talk you out of a cup of that coffee I smell?"

"Luke!" she yelled, surprised at the sight of him standing there. "You shouldn't sneak up on a person like that."

He gave a little laugh. "I didn't mean to scare you, Loraine." Motioning with a hand for her to come nearer, he said, "Help me over to that chair yonder at the table."

"You think you're strong enough to be out of bed?" she asked. Then lifting his right arm, she put it around her neck and helped him toward the table.

"If I wasn't I'd still be in there."

"Luke, you better watch your tone," she said with a playful frown. "You're in no shape to be getting smart-mouth with me." She helped him down into the chair. Stepping to the stove, she poured him a hot cup of coffee and set it on the table in front of him.

He picked it up and gave it a taste. "Now that's what I call good coffee," he said with a nod. Then he let out a long, ragged breath. "That was kinda silly on my part— taking on those McKuens the way I did. They almost did me in."

"Yeah," Loraine replied, taking a seat. "And if Paw hadn't got you out of there when he did, they would have too. You would have never made it, Luke. You'd lost too much blood."

He nodded. "He saved my bacon, that's for sure. I sure do want to thank 'im for doing it, but he put you and your maw in a lot of danger bringing me here." Luke paused for a moment, rubbing at the pain in his leg. Looking back, he asked, "Who was that other gent that helped you and Cork get me back in bed the other day?"

"Oh, that was my Uncle Elam—Paw's brother. He's out there riding the hills now watching for Laughlin's men. He figures they'll be coming soon."

"Elam Langtry?" Luke asked. "The Cavalry scout?"

"Yes," Loraine answered. "You know 'im?"

"Well, I don't know 'im," Luke admitted. "But I've for sure heard of 'im."

Loraine smiled. "He came riding in right after Maw died."

"Your maw's dead?" Luke asked, looking over surprised. "How did that happen?"

"She got the fever. We lost her five years ago this spring."

"I'm sorry, Loraine. I know how close you two were. I guess her passing took a lot out of your paw?"

"Yes, it did, Luke," Loraine answered through wet eyes. "Losing Mama almost killed 'im. He ain't been the same since. He's harder now, Luke. He's not the same man you knew." Loraine sipped at her coffee, then added, "But, anyway, Uncle Elam showed up a few days after the funeral, and he's been here ever since."

Suddenly Luke's face twisted from a sharp pain in his side, and he moaned. "Whew, that hurts." Giving his head a hard nod, he said, "But it's a sight better than it was a day or two ago. At least I'm able to move my arm a little."

"You're getting better," Loraine answered. "And your awful lucky that bullet in your leg didn't break a bone." She pushed up from the table, and asked, "You hungry? I've got some stew I can heat up."

He nodded his head yes. "And I'd take another cup of that coffee, too."

At the stove she added wood and moved the big black pot over the flames; taking up the coffeepot, she filled his cup. "Luke, what are we going to do?" she asked worriedly. "When they come? Laughlin's men, I mean." She shook her head. "You're in no shape to fight, and Paw and Uncle Elam can't hold that whole bunch off by themselves. Laughlin's hired those four gunfighters that I know of, and there's no telling how many more he's got back in town or on their way to Rising Star from somewhere else."

"Your right, Loraine," Luke admitted quietly. "I couldn't put up much of a fight in the shape I'm in. I need to get away from here, and away from Rising Star for a while. I need to go somewhere—a place where Laughlin's men can't find me. I need time for my wounds to heal and to get my strength back. I can't stay here, you know that. They'll be coming, Loraine, and when they do it'll be hell to pay."

She gave a understanding nod, and started to speak, but hearing the sudden sound of unexpected footsteps on the porch, her words stopped and her pulse quickened.

Luke, hearing the footsteps too, jerked his head in the direction of the door. At the same time, he dropped his hand for his gun, but felt nothing. Glancing down, he remembered—he had left it hanging over the back of a chair in the bedroom. A wave of uncertainty washed over him, and as he tried to stand, pain from the wounds brought him to an abrupt, agonizing stop. He glanced at Loraine, then back to the door; the latch moved and it started to open.

"Paw," Loraine said, seeing who it was. "What are you doing home?"

"Girl, I live here! I come and go as I see fit." Looking to the injured man, Cork asked, "What are you doing out of bed? You finally decide to wake up?"

Luke, hearing the questions, forced a faint smile and gave his head a nod. "Yeah, thought I might see if you've got some really mean horses I can ride this morning."

The old man gave a laugh. Then making his way to the table, he dropped to a chair. "Loraine," he said. "Get me a cup of that coffee there."

"Okay, Paw," she answered, turning toward the stove.

"Cork, I sure do want to thank you for helping me out the way you did."

"No thanks needed," the old man replied. "It's not over with yet, Luke. I just got back from town. Old Radford's got three warrants out on you for murder."

"Murder," Luke echoed. "Heck, Cork, Leroy Radford and his deputy was standing right there when it all took place; they know first-hand it was self-defense."

Cork tasted his coffee. Glancing back up, he asked, "What did happen, Luke? Didn't you know you couldn't take all of those McKuens on by yourself?"

Luke nodded, and after letting out a long, ragged sigh, he said, "I don't know what came over me, Cork. My mind for some reason just quit working. I wanted to kill Laughlin so bad that's all I could think of. My mind went blank to everything else—to my own safety or to getting away or anything like that. I did have a plan though; I had old Mousy tied to that big cottonwood down by the bridge, but when I got shot up so bad, that kinda all went out the window. They had me, Cork; if you hadn't come along when you did, I would have never made it. I'd lost too much blood . . . . I'd gotten into town just four days before, and had been talking to first one, then another—asking questions about how Paw got killed, and it became clear to me, after talking to old Smitty down at the livery, that Laughlin had ordered him killed and the McKuens had carried it out. Maxwell Laughlin is wanting the town, Cork, and to get it he's got to have control of the water."

"I kinda had the notion that's what it was, but didn't know for sure," Cork cut in. "They laughed 'im right out of the town meetin' that night, after he wanted the name of the town changed to Maxwell."

"That's what it is, all right," Luke replied. "And he'll do whatever it takes to get his hand on it. But anyway, to get back to my story—I knew the McKuens were watching me and had been ever since I rode into town, because every time I looked around I could see one of 'em. If it wasn't Barton or Quint standing there, it was Clint, Robert, or Porter. I knew my time was running out. After making up my mind what needed to be done—that Laughlin had to die—I went back to the hotel and waited until dark. When the sun had set, I saddled Mousy and led 'im down to the creek and tied 'im off to that big cottonwood there by the bridge and started back toward the Driftwood.

"That's when I saw Porter duck into the alley alongside the hotel. On up the street, Clint was making his way along the boardwalk in front of the general store and stopped when he saw me. I knew then that it was a trap—that I'd never make it to the door of the saloon. That's when I heard a gun from somewhere behind me fire and the bullet ripped at my left arm.

"I went to the ground, and when I looked up Porter was

running from the alley with his pistol raised, but he was a mite too slow. I shot him through the gut. I heard another shot from behind me and it went into the ground just a couple of inches to my right, and while getting to my feet I turned and let two quick shots go in that direction.

"I remember stumbling, and staggering toward the boardwalk. I glanced up the street toward the general store where Clint had been standing but saw nothing. I tried to shake the pain from my arm but it wouldn't move, and the half-hearted attempt just made the pain grow bigger. I made my way on along the boardwalk, stopping directly across from where I'd last seen Clint. There behind some boxes and sacks, I watched and waited, but saw or heard nothing. But then when I started across the street, Clint came from shadows of the doorway with his gun blazing. That's when I shot 'im between the eyes but before he fell he got off one more shot that hit me in the side. I turned at the sound of another shot that struck the ground at my feet, to see Robert had stood up from behind a water trough. I saw his pistol flash fire again at the same instant I pulled the trigger on mine. I turned and dove for cover; that's when the bullet struck me in the leg. I went down again, then I remember clawing and kicking at the ground and ending up under the barbershop—that's it.

"I never saw Barton or Quint until well after the shootin' was over, but I figure it was those two who was doing the shootin' at me from behind." He turned up an eye to Cork and concluded, "You know more about the next two weeks than I do."

A loud, shaky sigh escaped Loraine's trembling lips. "Do you want some stew, Paw?" she asked.

"Yeah, now that sounds like it might just hit the spot," Cork replied. Looking back to Luke, he added, "You know we can't stay here. The towns full of hired guns, and they'll be coming, Luke. You're in no shape to fight, and me and Elam can't hold 'em off by ourselves—there's just too many of 'em."

"I know," Luke answered. "Me and Loraine was just talking 'bout that. But I don't know where I can go, to where they can't find me. Maybe over to Caster. I know the Blacks over there. Maybe old Kelm will put me up for a while till I get back on my feet."

Cork shook his head. "You can't go to Caster, Luke. The streets are crawling thick with Laughlin's men over there too."

"Hey, wait a minute," Luke said. "Does that old Indian, Two Toes, still live up on Beaver Mountain?"

"I don't know if he does or not, to tell you the truth. I ain't seen 'im around here since late last winter when he came by a couple of times and I gave 'im a few things," Cork answered. After giving himself a little time to think, he added, "That would be a good place—a man can see a far piece in either direction from there." He pushed up to his feet. "I'll talk to Elam about it when he shows up, but right now, boy, you need to rest." Turning, he said, "Loraine, help me get 'im back in there on the bed."

A short time later, Cork returned to the chair at the table and Loraine went back to her work. No words were spoken for a long while, then Cork suddenly broke the silence. "It might get awful rough around here, Loraine," he said with a hard shake of his head. "Maybe you should think about going in to town to Mrs. Bitters and staying for a while. She's got a spare bedroom since that son of hers moved out. And I'm sure she wouldn't mind a bit—matter of fact, she'd probably enjoy your company."

"Oh, no, Paw, I don't want to go into town. I need to

stay out here with you and Uncle Elam, where I can look after Luke. If I'm gone, who's going to look after him?"

"Dang it, Loraine, we may have to drag out of here, girl, and we might have to do it in a hurry—in the cover of darkness and with a lot of shootin' going on. I just don't want you gettin' hurt." He turned a tired eye in her direction. "You and Elam are all I've got left."

She started across the floor toward where her father sat, with the thought of giving him a hug and telling him all was going to be just fine, when the report of a distant rifle stopped her.

The old man jumped to his feet. "They're coming—Loraine, they're coming." He reached down and took his pistol from the holster! "Here, you take this handgun and get in there with Luke and don't come out until the shootin' stops. If anybody tries to come through that door, you kill 'em."

She took the gun, but turning, she walked to the window and drew back the curtains. "I can't do any good in there, Paw. If they get by you and Uncle Elam, I don't stand much of a chance anyway."

He smiled. "You're just like your mother, God bless her heart. She never listened to me either." Giving his head a hard nod, he said, "Well, if you're going to stay, grab hold of the table there and help me move it over by the window and turn it up on its side."

They quickly moved the table in place and turned it up and after kneeling behind it, Cork carefully raised his head and looked out but saw nothing. Moments went by; then two more gunshots was heard and moments later another. "I wonder what's going on out there," he muttered to himself quite loud. Looking over, he said, "Loraine, I'm going to the barn. When I'm out the door I want you to put the bar in place and don't open it for anybody, you understand?"

She nodded her head. "Be careful, Paw."

But just as he got to his feet, he heard a horse coming fast. Looking out the window, he saw Elam riding hard from the south. The sight of his brother brought a nervous smile to his face. Stepping across to the door, Cork opened it and walked out. "What happened?" he called out as the dun came to a sliding stop.

"Had me a little run-in with some of Laughlin's men over yonder on that hill," Elam said, walking up. "Killed two of 'em. One got away. He'll be back, Cork, but I doubt if he'll be alone."

"Was it the McKuens?"

"No, it wasn't. I don't know who they were. I'd never seen either one of 'em before. But they were Laughlin's men; make no mistake 'bout that. They've been camped up there watching the house, and from the looks of the camp they've been there for several days."

Cork turned back toward the door. "Well, I guess we'd better get ready."

"There's no gettin' ready, Cork; there's just too many of 'em. Stayin' here would be suicide. How's Luke doing? Can he travel?"

"He's been up talking," Cork replied. "But traveling I imagine would be awful rough on 'im."

"Stayin' here well be rough on 'im too. We've got to go, Cork; that's all there is to it. Now you and Loraine get packed up and get Luke ready to travel while I hitch up the buckboard. And be quick about it; we ain't got much time."

Cork turned for the door but suddenly stopped and looked back at his brother. "There's an old Indian living in a cave up on Beaver Mountain; I'm almost sure he'll let us hole up there a few days. He don't take to white folks much, but I help 'im out a little from time to time when the weather turns bad with some flour and pork."

"I've seen 'im around here a time or two; that's where we'll head," Elam replied. Turning, he started across the yard in the direction of the barn.

Walking through the door, Cork said, "Loraine, get—"

"I heard Paw," she interrupted. "I'm already loading supplies into a sack."

Maxwell Laughlin sat slouched in the big leather chair behind his desk at the Driftwood Saloon. He was a large man with wide, powerful, thick shoulders, and dark, narrow eyes that were cold and hard. He had a full shock of neatly trimmed silver-gray hair that he kept oiled and combed over to the side, and a full, thick beard and mustache and coarse, bushy brows of the same silver-gray color. He was a man of few morals—a quick-tempered man to those around him that he knew to be weaker than himself, a man who had no qualms when it came to having someone killed who stood in the way of him getting what he wanted, be it man, woman or child—a man who no matter where he went seemed to make few friends and many enemies. He shook the last few drops from the whiskey bottle into his glass. Turning up an eye he called out in a loud, harsh voice, "Radford! Go out front and get us another bottle."

"Can't you send someone else, Mr. Laughlin? It just don't look right, me running errands and such—after all, I'm the sheriff."

Laughlin's body stiffened. "You'll do what I tell you to do or you won't be doing nothing—you'll be dead!" he shouted. Then after giving the man a long, cold stare, he said, "Just remember, Leroy, you're only the sheriff because I let you be the sheriff, and you're alive because I let you live. Now if you know what's good for you, you'll get out there and bring me a bottle like I told you to."

"Okay, okay," Radford replied nervously. "I just thought—"

"Don't think." Laughlin snorted. "Your thinking gets you in trouble and is the very reason Luke Ludd's not dead right now. If you'd just done what I told you to do, you and that half-wit Porter, I wouldn't be having the problems I'm having now—but no, you had to think. How much thinking does a man have to do to shoot another man in the back?" Laughlin slid his chair back and quickly sprang to his feet. "You're a sniveling coward, Radford. I know it and so do you—hell, the whole town knows it. If you wasn't you wouldn't let me or any other man talk to you this way." He threw the tail of his coat back and positioned his hand over the butt of his six-gun. "Now what's it going to be? You can either go after the bottle like I told you to do or fill you hand; it's up to you. It don't make me one bit of difference."

The man's face went instantly pale with fear. "Now, there's no need in all of that, Mr. Laughlin. I'm going; I'm on my way right now. I just thought you might want to send someone else, that's all."

"No, I don't want to send anyone else. I want you to do it, Sheriff Radford. And while you're out there tell Frank Clancy, Heath Benson, and Bill Powers to come in here. I need to talk to 'em."

"Yes, sir," Radford replied, looking back from the door.

Laughlin dropped back down to his chair, then looking across, he jerked his head toward the door and said, "When this is over, we won't need Radford or his deputy anymore.

And for sure I don't need Barton or Quint hanging around. Those two are the only ones left who know what really happened out at Luther's place."

Roscoe Nash slowly rubbed his mustache down and gave it a careful twist on the ends. Then taking a sip of his drink, he sat the glass down on the desk, looked over, gave his shoulders a shrug, smiled, and said, "Okay, that's up to you, Laughlin, but it'll cost you five hundred more."

Laughlin jerked his wallet from the inside pocket of his coat, counted out five hundred dollars, and pitched it down on the table. At the sound of the door opening, he looked up.

"Radford said you want to see us," Powers said, leading the other two men through the door.

"Yes, I do—" Laughlin started, but his comments were cut short by another man walking in. "Shane, what the blazes do you want?" Laughlin asked. "You're s'posed to be out there with Jack and Billy watching the Langtry house."

"We were, Mr. Laughlin, but something went wrong Jack and Billy are both dead. That old scout Elam Langtry killed 'em both."

Laughlin's face grew instantly dark with hatred; his eyes went hard, and after a moment, he said, "Okay, men, it's time. I want Luke Ludd found and when you find 'im if he ain't already dead I want you to kill 'im. And I want those Langtrys dead too—every last one of 'em, the girl and all." Looking back, he said, "Shane, you go down to the Ann Mayre and get Barton and Quint; tell 'em I need to see 'em right away."

"Okay, Mr. Laughlin," the man said as he turned for the door.

When he had gone, Laughlin looked to Roscoe Nash and

said, "As soon as you get that yellow-bellied coward out of town, kill 'im."

Roscoe nodded his head and, with the rest of the men following, walked through the door. Out on the boardwalk they waited for Shane to return with Barton and Quint, and when they arrived, they all mounted and rode out of town headed north.

Chapter Three

The two men, with Loraine's help, carried Luke from the house and put him in the back of the buckboard, laying him gently atop the patchwork quilt covering the soft layer of hay that had been put down. Taking up another blanket, Loraine shook it loose and spread it over him. With that done, she stepped from the buckboard and ran back into the house looking to make sure she'd gotten everything she had packed. When satisfied all had been loaded, she made her way back out the door, closing it behind her.

Her Uncle Elam was walking back from the barn where he'd gone to open the gates to let the livestock and chickens out. And her paw was headed in the direction of the hog-pen. When he got there, Sadie met him with her usual on-slaught of defiant grunts and squeals, snapping her teeth together with unbelievable force. Cork opened the gate and as she came out it, he stepped over the fence into her pen and closed the gate behind her, keeping the fence between them. The old black sow spun, rooting and snapping at the board trying to get at the man. But seeing that he had tricked her once again, she turned and headed off down the hill in a trot toward the creek. After she had gone, Cork swung open the gates to the other two pens and started back toward the house. "I guess we're ready," he said.

"Okay, Cork," Elam replied. "You and Loraine light a shuck. I'm going to stay behind for a bit. I put Luke's saddle there in the back of the wagon and before I head out I'll swing by and get his horse."

"You'll be coming before long, then?" Cork asked.

Elam nodded his head and said, "Yeah, I'll catch up somewhere along the trail." Taking Loraine by the arm, he helped her up into the seat.

Cork led his horse around to the back of the buckboard and tied him off to the tailboard. Stepping back around, he climbed up the side to the seat, and with a hard nod to his brother, flipped the reins and started the team. But at the big oak tree where his wife Estelle was buried, Cork drew up and stepped to the ground. Removing his hat, he walked slowly toward the cross-shaped marker and dropped down to one knee, and in that position he stayed for a long moment. Then standing, he made his way back toward the wagon, wiping at his eyes. After crawling back into the seat, he tipped his hat in the direction of the grave, lightly flipped the reins, and started the team again.

Loraine turned in the seat and threw up a good-bye hand to her Uncle Elam, and he waved back. Letting her eyes fall upon the little white house in which she had been born and had lived all her life, she wondered if she'd ever see it again.

Elam stood watching until the buckboard went over the rise out of sight. Crossing to the barn, he took up the lead ropes of the three horses he'd left tied at the corral fence. Walking back to his horse, he gathered the reins and stepped into leather. Turning, he led the horses north along the same trail the wagon had just traveled, for four, maybe five hundred yards, then swinging around, he led them back to the house and in doing so trampled out all signs of wagon tracks. At the hitch rail, he let the four horses stand, making sure they marked the ground good with their feet.

Riding from there, he led them along the trail leading south. At the south fork of Dead Cow Creek, he drew up and let the horses drink and when they'd had their fill, he touched the dun with a easy spur and crossed the slow moving water and continued on south to where the trail forked. There, he drew up again and sat, listening—watching along the left trail in the direction of Rising Star, but he saw or heard nothing. Touching the dun forward, he swung onto the right trail toward Caster and continued on in that direction for better than a mile.

Coming to a wide, wind-swept, rocky flat, he drew up again. This time, he stepped to the ground and threw back the flap on his saddlebag and took out the four pieces of burlap he had cut from a feed sack, and some string. Wrapping each hoof of the dun with the burlap, he tied it in place. Taking the lead ropes off the other three horses, he stepped back into leather, and waving his arms high in the air, he hollered, shooing the three horses on west toward Caster. With that done, Elam swung the dun north, and rode at a canter across the rocky flat to where four or five oak saplings grew bunched and twisted from nothing more than a crack in the rock. Making his way around them, he rode on across the slick, wind-swept rock to a place where the trail fell away sharply.

The dun balked, not wanting to go any futher; he bowed

his neck, perked his ears, and gave a loud blow. Elam spurred at the horse's sides forcing him off into the narrow, deep cut. The left stirrup scraped hard on the rock wall and the right one dangled empty, for Elam had removed his foot from it and bringing up his leg, crossed it over the pommel. The dun, walking on delicate feet, went on down the narrow path to a place some twenty yards along where the trail leveled out somewhat and widened enough for Elam to step to the ground. Dropping the reins, he made his way quickly back along the trail, and breaking a limb from down low on a scurb cedar, he brushed out his tracks. Climbing back in the saddle, he rode on, but he had not ridden far when the trail fell away again and narrowed to a width that he was not sure the dun could squeeze through.

Knowing there was no turning back, Elam stepped to the ground and raising the stirrups, he hung them over the pommel. Tailing the reins, he led the horse slowly into the mouth of the narrow opening. At one point, where the walls closed in to their narrowest, the dun balked again, but with Elam talking to him and urging him on by pulling on the reins, the horse suddenly lunged forward just barely making it through but not without losing a little hair on either side. They made their way on down to a place where the trail was covered with lose gravel, and the dun on nervous feet scrambled across. Then working their way through an outcropping of boulders they came to the bottom where the oak once again grew tall and thick. He took to the trees easing his way back along the ridge toward the house.

He had not traveled far when the distant sound of several horses at a gallop got his attention. Swinging at right angle, he rode to within a stone's throw of the edge of the ridge. Stepping to the ground, he quickly tied the horse and, reaching over the saddle, he slipped the Winchester from its boot and walked hunkered down among the rocks and trees until he could look upon the shadow darkened trail. Gazing south, he saw what he thought to be eight, maybe ten men, riding along in a tight bunch. At that distance and in the dim light of the late evening, he could not make out who they were, but he did not have to see their faces, because in the back of his mind, he already knew.

He had not planned on Nash and his bunch of killers showing their hand until morning, when they'd have plenty of time to kill, and the light needed to hunt a person down if someone happened to get away. Coming this late in the day only showed their appetite for blood and their eagerness to kill and destroy, and Maxwell Laughlin's unwillingness to wait any longer.

Elam eased back through the trees to where the dun stood tied. Stepping into leather, he made his way on north along the ridge, riding parallel to his soon-to-be pursuers. Coming to the creek, he drew up and sat listening for the splash that would tell him they were crossing the creek, but instead they swung east and moments later their hoof beats faded along the trail in that direction.

They're going to wait until morning, Elam thought to himself. "That's your first mistake, Nash," he whispered under his breath. "Maybe your last. Because I'll kill you in the morning if I can." Crossing the creek, he rode on, wanting to get in position, knowing that if he could only take Nash out of the picture, their fastest gun and best tracker would be no more. With that thought in mind, he rode on through the blackness to about the area where he had killed the two men this morning. He looked in the direction of where he knew the house to be but saw nothing but darkness, and knowing he needed to be within one hundred and fifty yards for a good easy shot, he rode on for another little bit. Then hearing the not-too-distant sound of the barn door squeaking as it worked back and forth on its hinges in the breeze, he drew up and sat listening, and when satisfied that all sounds were accounted for, he slid to the ground and stripped the saddle from the dun. Leading him to a little clearing where beams of moonlight penetrated the thick canopy above the spotted ground, he put the hobbles on, and the horse dropped his head and went to nibbling at the tender green grass. Back at the saddle, he took a piece of jerky from the saddlebags, a blanket from his bedroll, and his Winchester from its boot; he worked his way back toward the ridge and under the low hanging limbs of a large old oak, he dropped crossed legged to the ground. He sat chewing on the jerky, his ears listening, his eyes searching the darkness near and far, then he saw it—the dim flicker from a distant campfire. He pulled the blanket up over his shoulders, and leaning back he closed his eyes.

"How's he doing?" Cork asked, glancing back through the darkness at his daughter.

"Not too good, Paw," Loraine answered. "He's awful hot—he's got a terrible fever."

"There's a creek just on up the trail a little way," Cork replied. "We'll pull up there and rest and let the horses drink. Maybe build a fire, make some coffee, and eat a bite. You hungry?"

"I'm hungrier than a she-wolf nursing a litter of pups," Loraine answered.

Her paw laughed. "Now I'd say that's getting pretty hungry, girl," he said, looking back, but in the darkness, he could not see her beautiful smiling face. But he knew she was there and that she was smiling. Loraine was so much like her maw. In her looks and in the way she carried herself and in many of the things she said and did—just like her. He didn't know where she came up with some of the sayings she had, but her maw was the same way. Just when you didn't think there was any reason in the world to laugh, she'd say or do something silly and for that instant your problems were gone. He reached up and wiped a tear of memory from his eye and whispered, "I love you, Estelle— I mean, Loraine."

There was a short silence then the words. "We know you do, Paw," Loraine replied from the darkness. "And we love you too."

At the creek Cork built a small fire and started a pot of coffee and sliced bacon into a pan. Loraine bathed Luke's wounds with cool water from the creek and gave him a dose of laudanum. Just for a brief moment, he had regained consciousness but did not speak before drifting back off to sleep.

"Loraine," Cork called out. "Supper's ready."

"Okay, Paw, I'll be right there," she answered, stepping from the back of the buckboard; crossing to the fire, she took the plate he handed her. "How much further do you reckon it is to where we're going, Paw?"

"Another ten, maybe twelve miles I'd say, maybe a mite further."

"I wonder what Uncle Elam's doing? Where's he at? I figured he would have caught up with us by now."

"I don't know," Cork answered worriedly. "But there's one thing about your Uncle Elam, girl, if he ain't already dead, and I sure hope he ain't, he's either causin' 'em hell or fixin' to." He gave a worried chuckle. "Yes, sir, I'd hate to be in them there fellers' boots." Standing, he kicked dirt on the fire, reducing the remaining few flames to just light puffs of white-gray smoke. Gesturing with a hand toward a blanket, he added, "You better try to get some rest, Loraine; we'll be moving out before long." Stepping across to where his shotgun leaned against a stump, he took it up and started back down the trail.

"Where you going, Paw?"

"You don't worry, Loraine," he answered, walking away. Stopping, he looked back and said, "You just rest now, it'll be daylight before long." Turning, he walked on disappearing into the hazy blur of the night.

The nearby rustling of leaves brought Elam's mind awake but left his eyes closed. He listened more closely, and when he had determined the sounds were made by animal, he opened his eyes slowly to see nothing but night. Hearing several loud, popping sounds, he looked in that direction to see only a flash of white. Then he heard a low grunt, and at that moment, he finally realized what it was that was making the noise and what he was looking at. His pulse quickened and his throat grew instantly tight. Not twenty feet away old Sadie stood looking straight at him. He tightened his grip on the stock of the Winchester lying across his lap, moving his finger over the trigger. But quickly realizing that he could not afford to shoot her, for the men across the way would surely hear the gunshot, he released his grip and slowly moved his hand down to his left side until it came in contact with the curved deer horn that made up the handle on his knife.

The air lay still along the ridge, and had a heavy, muggy feel, and no leaves moved among the trees. Sweat ran freely down his face and had soaked through his shirt front and back. He wanted desperately to wipe the salty sting from his eyes, but knowing that any movement might cause Sadie to attack, he sat motionless resisting the urge.

Suddenly, she let out a loud squeal and charged but had only taken a couple of steps when she stuck her front feet hard into the ground and came to a sliding stop.

Elam, figuring—hoping—she was bluffing, sat not moving a muscle.

The hog stood, popping her teeth together, looking straight at him for a long moment. Then turning, she walked off a little way and stretched out under the low-hanging limbs of a nearby mesquite bush.

You're just waiting for me to make a move, ain't you, old gal? Elam thought to himself, looking through the now dim light at the massive pile of black muscle. *You're going to get what you want, but I sure don't think you're going to like it none.* Slowly letting his eyes move back east, he looked in the direction of the house and could barely make out that its outline and the barn's too were starting to emerge from the darkness. From the chicken coop a rooster crowed, and across the way another answered him.

Letting his eyes move more east, he searched for and found the flicker of the distant campfire, but now it glowed more brightly, telling him that it had been newly stoked and the would-be killers probably sat around it drinking coffee. *I sure wish I had a little coffee,* he thought to himself. Then he glanced back to where the old hog had bedded down. She lay relaxed with one eye looking at him. *More than that, I wish she was gone. I need to be saddling my horse; they'll be coming before long and I need to be ready. I can wait, I guess, and when they ride into the yard I can shoot her, then try to get a shot at Roscoe before he realizes what's going on, but I'd still have to find and saddle my horse and that would make me too late. They would have me. No, I need to get rid of the hog first, before they come.*

He looked back in the direction of the house and barn;

the livestock for the most part had returned to the lots; even the three horses he had shooed along the trail toward Caster had returned and stood waiting for their morning feeding. The old milk cow mingled aimlessly in the yard with chickens picking at the ground around her feet. Her bag was full and tight—she needed to be milked and her little spotted calf, after having its fill, lay in the flower bed at the end of the porch.

At the hogpen some of the pigs ran and played and at the feed barrel two sows worked at trying to get to the feed inside. One rooted at the bottom; the other reared to its side, causing the barrel to sway, almost tipping it over. Not realizing how close she had come to getting what she wanted, she dropped her feet back to the ground.

Out of the corner of his eye, Elam caught a glimpse of something flicker. Letting his eyes swing around, he saw the group of men riding from the east. He quickly looked back to see Sadie had gotten to her feet; apparently she had seen him move. At that instant, she grunted and snapped her teeth together. The hair along her back was bristled, and Elam knew when she came this time it wouldn't be a bluff. He gripped the stock of the rifle and started to stand, when all of a sudden the hogs at the barn went to squealing. Elam looked to see the barrel laying on its side and the hogs moving in on the spilled grain.

Sadie's head came up with her ears perked, and without giving the man a second look she headed down the hill toward the house. Elam wasted no time in springing to his feet, and almost in a dead run he made his way to where his saddle lay. Taking up the bridle, he walked hurriedly toward the little clearing where he'd left the dun.

Hearing, then seeing, the man approach, the horse raised his head and gave a nicker. Elam quickly put his hand over the horse's nose to keep him quiet, and while speaking to him quietly, he slipped the bit into his mouth, taking the headstall up over his head. He removed the hobbles, and leading the horse back to where the saddle lay, he threw it on and after working it down in place, he laced the latigo through the rings and drew tight on the cinch.

Now, he was ready. He looked back to the east to see the men had crossed the creek and had quickened their pace to a canter. It would not be long now. Reaching, he took up the Winchester, and after slipping the thong from over the hammer of his six-gun, he loosened it in the holster. Now all he needed to do was wait for Roscoe Nash to give him a shot. He dropped cross-legged to the ground in among an outcropping of rocks; he removed his hat, placing it on the ground beside him. Then wiping his palms on the front of his shirt, he blinked the sweat from his eyes. It was time to deal the cards.

Looking east, and a little south, he saw the group of men as they rode from a stand of oak. *But wait a minute,* he thought to himself after getting a good look. *That's not Roscoe out front—that's Heath Benson.* He looked more closely but Roscoe Nash was not riding with the men. Elam let his eyes move quickly along the trail the men had traveled but saw nothing of Roscoe or his horse. Then letting his gaze scan slowly over the ridge to the east and seeing no sign of the man he looked for, he quickly glanced along the rocky ridge on which he sat both to his left and to his right but again saw nothing. "Now I wonder what he's up to?" Elam mumbled to himself. "Or more important, where he's at." He knew it was not like a man of Nash's character to stay in town while the grand finale was taking place; he would want to be leading men—giving the orders. He'd want to be in command. Had he sensed something? Elam thought to himself. Maybe he had figured on there being an ambush from somewhere and was lying in wait, to see where the shots came from. Elam knew Nash to be a smart man; he had to be to live this long in his line of work, but was he that smart? After giving the ridge another good look, Elam turned his attention back upon the group of men. *If I can't kill Roscoe, then who will it be?* The other three men that made up the Nash gang were all men of about the same character. Frank Clancy, Elam had heard, was faster than a rattlesnake with a pistol and a dead shot from any position. On the other hand, Bill Powers, Elam had been told, was a mite slower with his six-gun than Frank was, but more brutal and more apt to shoot a man in the back and had been thought by many a lawmen to have done just that on any number of occasions. By all accounts, Bill Powers, behind Roscoe Nash, was the bad one. Elam eyed the man as he rode by. Then turning his attention to the man leading the group, he saw a man that he'd heard very little about. Heath Benson was not as well known as the other three but still undoubtedly dangerous. The one thing Elam had heard about him made his blood boil; apparently he enjoyed tormenting women and when he was done with them he'd slit their throat. Sometimes he used some other means to take their lives, but usually it was his preference to end their pleas for mercy and tears with a knife.

The other four men were really out of place riding with this bunch; Barton and Quint had both, along with their three brothers whom Luke killed, bullied the people of Rising Star for years and they both were known to be fast with their guns. But not near fast enough to ride with the likes of Roscoe Nash and his bunch, they were probably being used as nothing more than pawns. Men to do the dirty work, and at the end they would be discarded like so much trash in a wash or gully somewhere, left to the hungry mouths of the coyotes and buzzards.

The other two men he didn't know; one he had never seen before and had no idea where he'd come from. Probably nothing more than a cowhand wanting to ride with a bad bunch. But the other man, the one with the corn-colored hair, Elam recognized as being the one who had just by the skin of his teeth escaped from this very ridge with his life yesterday morning. And if not for a tree getting in the way as Elam pulled off the shot, he would have never made it, but apparently not being satisfied with his good fortune, he had made the mistake of coming back for more.

Where the trail turned leading up to the house, the men drew their horses in to a walk. Three turned and rode around coming up to the house from behind. The other four rode steadily across the yard where they drew up at the hitch rail. "Hello in the house," Benson called out, then after a short impatient pause, he asked, "Cork, you in there?" He sat with his hands resting on the pommel. "Cork, if you're in there you better come out with your hands up, and bring that pretty, sweet thing you call a daughter out with you. And if Ludd's in there, bring 'im out too."

"Ain't nobody in there," Frank snarled. "They've already drug out."

"I figure you're right, Frank," Heath replied. "Okay, a couple of you men check the house and barn, the rest of you get to looking for tracks." He gave a laugh. "We've got some killing to do, men. But if you find the girl don't kill her; bring her to me. I'll take care of her."

At Benson's last words, a wave of hatred washed over Elam, and he swung the Winchester up to his shoulder.

Quickly looking down the barrel, he brought the man's chest in line with the sights and slowly tightened his finger on the trigger. But thinking, he relaxed. It wouldn't do any good if he got himself killed. No, he'd wait and do it as planned. He lowered the rifle back to its resting place across his lap and sat watching as the men searched the house and barn.

"Here they are," Frank called out, pointing along the trail leading south. "Four sets of tracks, it looks to me like; that means Ludd's with 'em." He stood looking south. "We know they didn't go to town, so I figure they're headed west to Caster—"

A loud squeal filled the morning air, then a man's horrifying scream. Elam cast his eyes north to see Sadie attacking one of the men, the one he had never seen before. The man was trying to draw his pistol, but she had his leg in her mouth, her powerful jaws crushing the bones, her razor-sharp teeth tearing at the man's flesh. All the helpless man could do was scream. The men all ran with their guns drawn in the direction of the vicious turmoil, but by the time they got to where they could get off a shot, Sadie had already ripped the leg from the man's body and had sunk her teeth into his belly, shaking him like a rag doll. Bill Powers pulled off a shot, striking her in the right shoulder. She staggered, squealing at the pain as the hot piece of lead entered her body. Turning, she charged at Bill with her mouth open. Powers fanned two more shots into her massive frame, but she kept coming, her teeth popping together harder than ever. Suddenly the morning air was filled with a hail of gunfire and the old black sow dropped to the ground. As life slipped away she tried to stand but Barton McKuen stopped the attempt with two more shots to her head.

"Help me. Somebody please help me," the mauled man pleaded. "I need a doctor bad," he moaned, while holding his hands over his belly, trying to keep his guts from coming out.

Benson glanced down at the man lying there. Turning to the one with corn-colored hair, he shook his head and said, "He can't be helped. Kill 'im."

"Wait, Benson. I don't want to kill 'im. He ain't done nothing to me."

Benson spun. "I'll shoot 'im myself then." Thumbing the hammer back, he let a round go into the man's head. Spinning back to the man with corn-colored hair, he fanned one into his chest.

The man staggered back on his heels, grabbing at his chest with both hands. A blank, stiff, pale look swept his face as he slowly crumbled to the ground.

"Hell, Benson," Barton called out. "What did you go and shoot Shane for?"

"He was a coward!" Benson shouted. "And Laughlin wanted 'im dead. Why, Barton? You thinkin' 'bout maybe gettin' in the game?

Barton forced a nervous smile. "No—no, I'm not," he answered, moving his hand away from his gun. "I was just wondering' why you shot 'im, that's all. He was nothin' to me."

"When you want in, Barton, just let me know," Benson snarled. "I'll be more than happy to oblige."

"Benson," Frank cut in. "We've got a job to do."

Heath Benson stood with his feet spread, his hand resting over the butt of his Colt. "What's it going to be?" he asked, his eyes locked in a cold, killing stare on Barton's.

Barton cast his eyes to the ground, shaking his head. "I don't have any fight with you, Benson," he said through pale, trembling lips; then shaking his head from side to side, he turned and walked slowly toward his horse.

Benson stepped up to leather. Swinging the horse, he rode to a clearing just south of the house; there he sat for a long moment looking east. Elam looked in the same direction but saw nothing. Was Benson giving Roscoe some kind of signal? Was Roscoe up there somewhere among the rocks and trees, waiting, watching? Elam let his eyes move slowly along the ridge again, but the present search revealed no more than the first. He glanced back to see the men had gathered at the hitch rail in front of the barn where the false trail started. "Let's go," Benson called out. "Roscoe will be meet us there where the trail forks." Swinging his horse, he led the men from the yard.

Elam readied the Winchester, knowing he needed to let them get far enough along the trail before he shot. They'd not know where the shot came from, and while they were down behind cover looking, and trying to figure it out, he'd make his escape.

The group of now just six men slowly made their way south, looking and pointing at the ground. They passed the fifty-yard mark unaware of what was fixing to happen; then at the hundred-yard mark Elam raised the rifle to his shoulder. Taking aim, he zeroed in on the middle of Bill Powers' back, but raising the barrel another couple of inches, he found the back of Heath Benson's head just over Bill's left shoulder. He steadied the gun and pulled the trigger. The bullet flew, finding its target with incredible force, snapping Benson's head forward; his eyes popped from their sockets as the bullet made its exit, but Benson was unaware because he was already dead. The men instantly dropped to the ground, running to take cover in behind rocks and trees.

Elam heard a loud swoosh, then a thud. Realizing it was a gunshot, he dove to his left head-first in behind a tree. Then looking east, he let his eyes move along the ridge and saw a puff of smoke. At the same instant, he heard the report of the rifle shot. "You son of a devil," he said under his breath. "I knew you were up there." He turned, and on all fours crawled another twenty or so feet. Standing, he walked hunkered down to where the dun stood tied. Stepping into leather, he swung the horse west and made his way toward the top of the ridge. Behind him were shouts and occasional gunfire, but he rode on knowing that no one except Roscoe had any idea of his location. After breaking over the top, he turned at left angle and rode south in the direction of Caster wanting his soon-to-be pursuers to think that was where he was headed. The dun was leaving no tracks to speak of because the burlap still covered his hooves, but he was marking the ground enough that a seasoned tracker like Roscoe would have very little trouble finding his trail. Elam rode on for about a mile; coming to a rocky plateau, he spurred the dun across it with the thought of riding south until he came to the next rocky ridge. There, he would turn west and ride in that direction for a bit then swinging back north, he would work around to where Luke's horse was staked out, then head on north. But noticing the dun had started to limp, and thinking he had probably just picked up a stone, Elam drew up and stepped to the ground. Hurrying around, he bent to pick up his right foot and that was when he noticed blood dripping from a hole in the horse's shoulder. The bullet that had been meant for him had hit the horse, and he was leaving a blood trail. Elam stood, looking north in the direction his pursuers would soon be coming. With the horse leaving a blood trail Roscoe would have no trouble in following it straight to him. After giving his situation some thought and realizing there were only a couple of things he could do, Elam jerked the knife from its scabbard and quickly dug the bullet out, and with that done, he stripped the saddle and bridle from the horse and gave him a hard slap on the hip. The horse lunged into a run, disappearing moments later into the trees on the far side of the plateau. Elam watched the dun go, knowing that Roscoe would stay with the blood trail until he found the horse, then he and the rest of the killers riding with him would be coming back.

Taking up the saddle, he started walking west, then dropped off the plateau into a dry creek bottom. He turned north knowing that the only two chances he had to escape now were to get back to the house where he hoped the horses would still be waiting for their morning feeding, or to the little grove of pecan trees where Luke's horse was. But he knew too, the time he had to do either of those things depended entirely on how far the blood trail the dun was leaving would lead Roscoe and his men away before they found him and started to backtrack.

With the added burden of the saddle swung over his shoulder, Elam walked on, his eyes watching for any movement, his ears keen to the slightest sound. Out away from the canopy of trees in which he made his way, the sun shined bright from among the big, puffy, white clouds that dotted the pale-blue sky, and the heat of the day was starting to build. Somewhere from overhead a hawk shrieked loud, and just above the treetops to the not-too-distant northeast a large number of buzzards was gathering, no doubt right over the house where the three men and old hog lay dead. And it was there he needed to go; if he could only make it back to the house maybe the horses would still be there. With that thought in mind, he adjusted the weight of the saddle, and with the other hand he mopped the sweat from his brow. Suddenly hearing what he thought to be a snort from a distant horse, his pulse quickened at the sound. Slowly he eased the saddle to the ground and walked to the foot of the steep bank. There, he quietly slid the action on the Winchester and started the short climb up the side, being very careful to place each foot so as not to dislodge a rock or anything else that might roll or slide giving away his position. Just before reaching the top, he removed his hat, hanging it over a nearby limb. Raising his eyes just barely above the edge of the creek bank, he slightly parted the yellowish, brown spines of a clump of short prairie grass and looked through. No more than forty yards away Roscoe led the men along the trail, his eyes watching the ground.

"That was one fine shot that old Roscoe made," Quint said, looking over at his brother.

"Close to four hundred yards, I reckon," Barton answered with a nod. "I wonder where he's hit?"

"You two stop your yapping!" Roscoe shouted. Turning his horse, he put a hard spur to his sides and rode back in their direction. "I want you two to shut your mouths. Y'all are 'bout as dumb as that dead hog lying back there, and if you don't shut up you're going to be in the same shape. *Good shot*—hell, I shot at a puff of smoke, that's all, and if you two would stop talking long enough to look down you'd see the man, whoever he is, ain't hit anywhere. The horse is the one that's hit," he said, pointing to a track on the ground. "He's limping on his right front foot—look down at the sign. Now shut up and come on and keep your eyes open or you'll end up with your head shot off like Heath lying back there."

"We didn't mean—" Barton started to say.

Roscoe jerked his head around. "Shut up. Not another word." Looking over at Bill Powers, he added, "If either one of those two make another sound, shoot 'em."

Bill nodded he would, then asked, "Who do you reckon it is doing all the shootin'—Luke?"

"Maybe. It might be that brother of Cork's—what's his name? That old tracker."

"Elam," Bill replied.

"Yeah, Elam," Roscoe echoed. "It might even be Cork, I don't know, but it looks to me like whoever it is, they're running scared and if that horse don't play out on 'im before he gets there, he's going to lead us straight to the rest of 'em." Touching the horse forward, he led the group on along the trail south.

Elam sat with his finger on the trigger watching them go and after they had, he slid back to the bottom. Taking up the saddle, he slung it back in place over his shoulder and headed on north. They might find the injured horse in just the next few minutes or it might take them a day or two, but on the latter he was not willing to stake his life.

By midafternoon, he had made it back to Dead Cow Creek where he dropped to his belly and drank his fill, and after wetting his bandanna in the cool water, he wiped at his face and neck. Standing, he let his eyes move slowly along the southern horizon in search of his pursuers, but after giving it a long hard look, he saw nothing. Feeling a hunger pain, he took a piece of jerky from his saddlebag and stuck it in his mouth. Picking up the saddle, he walked on knowing he was within a mile and a half of his destination.

By the time Elam had dropped off the ridge west of the house, the sun hung low in the distant sky and its reddish-orange rays shoved at the back of the ridge and trees pushing their shadows long, gray, and jagged to the east. He worked his way from among the oak-covered ridge just west of the barn and had to this point seen no sign of horses or livestock of any kind. The corral was empty. He had just started around the barn when he heard what he thought to be a horse hoof clicking stone. He jerked his head around looking south but saw nothing; he stood motionless, holding his breath trying to hear the sound again, but after a long moment of hearing nothing but silence, he walked on toward the door of the barn. Inside, he took a quick look but it, too, like the corral, was empty and the hopes he had of finding a horse was quickly dwindling. "That just leaves Luke's horse," he mumbled to himself. Turning, he started back toward the front, knowing he had another three long miles to walk, but just as he pushed the door open, he came face to face with something that made a rush of blood go to his head, causing him to instantly drop his hand for his gun. But realizing what he was looking at, he slowly stuck out his hand and spoke a soft, "Whoa." Standing before him was a horse and saddle apparently one belonging to one of the dead men. He gathered the reins and led the horse to where he'd left his own saddle. He was not long in switching them. Pulling the cinch tight he stepped in, and after giving one more quick look south, he swung the horse onto the trail leading north and rode off.

Chapter Four

"Whoa!" Cork called out to the team, as he drew in on the lines alongside a little creek just south of Beaver Mountain. Turning, he looked back at his daughter and said, "You wait here with Luke and the wagon, Loraine. I'll take my horse and ride on up and see if I can find Two Toes. He may not take a liking to us being here."

"Okay," Loraine answered. "But before you go, Paw, pull the wagon up over there in the shade of those two tall cottonwoods."

Cork, giving the reins a flip, moved the wagon into the coolness of the shade, but just as he stepped to the ground, he felt a rifle barrel push firmly against his back. "Two Toes, I sure hope that's you," he said, slowly raising his hands.

"What brings you here? Why do you come to Beaver Mountain?" the voice behind him asked.

"We've got a man there in the back that's hurt—he's got

bullet holes in 'im and we've got a gang of killers on our trail," Cork replied, letting his hands slowly drop. But after a hard nudge from the rifle barrel, he raised them back up high above his head.

At the sudden movement, Loraine's breath caught. "We don't want any trouble," she yelled. "We need a place that we can hole up a few days, that's all, just until Luke can travel." Gazing down she saw the image of a man that was nothing like what she had expected.

He stood dressed in a loose-fitting wolf-skin shirt and buckskin pants. He was a small man, short in stature with narrow, sloping shoulders. His face was thin and dark; his skin was darkened to a leather-brown color more from the Cheyenne blood running deep and proud in his veins then from the sun. The lines that cut deep across his forehead and along his eyes and mouth showed a man up in years. His nose was wide and flat and the corners of his mouth drooped down. His hair was long, but thinning and gray, and he wore it in long braids. Tied to the braid on the right side he wore an eagle feather hanging down—to his people, a symbol of honor and bravery.

He looked up hard into Loraine's pleading eyes. Thinking back to the winters that these people had given him flour, eggs, and meat, he lowered his gun and asked in a voice that cracked with age, "Why do you think they won't come here and find you?"

Cork shook his head. "By coming this far north, Two Toes. Maybe they'll think we've drug out and left the country. They'll have my place; it's what's they're really after. There's a man back in Rising Star by the name of Maxwell Laughlin; he's wanting to take over the town. And the only way he can do it is to get control of the land and water."

"That not concern me," Two Toes replied coldly.

Quickly looking at the man in the back of the wagon, he said, "He not look so good. Is that not the boy that grew up in the lodge made of rock west of yours?"

"Yes, it is," Cork answered with a nod. "Luke Ludd is his name. The men that's after us killed his pappy and shot him. They'll be looking to finish the job."

Two Toes turned from the wagon. "You can stay," he said in a low voice. "You help me, now I help you." Casting an eye toward the setting sun, he added, "It's too late to start up now. We wait till the sun comes again, but the wagon can't go. Will have to stay; trail not wide enough."

"We'll need to make a travois then," Cork said. "I'll do that while Loraine is cookin' us up some supper."

"I will not stay," Two Toes said, turning toward the mountain. "I go. Be back when the sun is there," he said, pointing just above the tree tops to the east. "You be ready."

"Okay," Cork replied, throwing up a good-bye hand. Helping Loraine from the wagon, he unhitched the team, drove picket pins, and tied the horses in a good stand of rich green grass within easy reach of water. They gathered wood for a fire, and while Loraine started supper, Cork walked to a stand of cottonwood and cut two tall straight saplings to make the litter. Later they sat by the fire with their plates of beans and fried bacon. "Paw," Loraine started. "How do you reckon Two Toes learned to talk English so good?"

"Well, it's hard to say, Loraine, but I've heard it told that he was raised by the soldiers over at Fort Richardson. Mackenzie and his troops raided a Cheyenne camp years ago somewhere up north from here. 'Course when the Indians saw 'em coming they lit out for the hills, but Two Toes's foot being clubbed the way it is, he couldn't keep up and was soon left behind. One of the soldiers found 'im hidin' in among some rocks where the boy's mother had left 'im, probably thinking about coming back for 'im after the soldiers had left. But Mackenzie, even as cold-hearted as he was, didn't want 'im to starve to death, so they loaded 'im up and took 'im back to the fort, and that's where he grew up." Cork paused, looking unknowingly at his daughter. "I don't know any of that to be true, Loraine, but that's what I've been told." He shook his head and gave a laugh. "After Two Toes got up in years, he went to scoutin' for 'em; he'd track the Comanches, Apaches, and the Kiowa— but he wouldn't track the Cheyenne, no, sir, he wouldn't track his own people and that caused 'im a lot of trouble. After he refused to do so, they locked 'im in the stockade, and months later after being released, he ran off and ended up here on this mountain, and here he still is."

"If he deserted, Paw," Loraine questioned, "I wonder why the Army didn't come looking for 'im?"

"It's hard to say, Loraine, why some people get by with doing things that would send others to jail, but some do. Maybe they figured he'd done enough, or maybe they figured it would be easier just to leave 'im alone than it would be to try to take 'im off this mountain." He suddenly stood up and handed Loraine his plate, then crossing to the buckboard, he took up his shotgun; glancing back, he said, "You better step about, Loraine, it'll be dark before long. You need to get the plates washed and Luke looked after, so you can put the fire out; we sure don't need anyone seeing it. I'm going to walk back down the trail a ways. You get some rest, and I'll see you at breakfast."

"Okay, Paw, you be careful."

Cork made his way along the trail, wanting to get far enough from camp and in a position that he would see

D.J. Bishop

anyone approaching well before they got in sight of the wagon. On the western horizon the sun was setting, its golden rays struggling for life, but it would soon fade, giving way to the darkness and uncertainty of the night. To the south a turkey gobbled, letting the hens know it was time to find a roost. And high in the trees above, the south wind stirred light and warm.

Cork made his way slowly along the east side of the brushy ridge, through a patch of oak saplings that grew thick, to a small outcropping of rocks concealed from above by the overhang of the ridge. Working his way in among those rocks, he took a seat concealed from all directions but with a clear view of the oak covered hills to the south and the trail they had traveled to get here. *I wonder where Elam is,* he thought to himself. *I figured he would have caught up with us by now.* But knowing his brother would never follow the same trail for fear of leading the killers straight to them, Cork let his tired eyes slowly move along the ridge to the distant east and after a careful study and seeing nothing, he laid the shotgun across his lap and settled in for the long night.

Hours later, he opened his eyes into a world of total darkness. Listening, he could hear no sound except for the trickle of water running over rocks in the creek a few yards behind him, and the rustle of leaves high in the trees as the cool night air made its way past. The coolness caused him to pull his collar tight to his neck. All of a sudden, from the distant north a coyote yapped his loneliness to the moon and from somewhere along the ridge to the south another immediately answered him. Other than those few sounds it was quiet, peaceful and dark—a darkness the eye could not penetrate. He could see no more with his eyes open than

he could with them closed. All he had to alert him of someone approaching was his ears, and he sat straining them,
trying to pick up the slightest sound of muffled voices, or
boots, or horse hooves walking over the loose gravel along
the ridge or the crunch the dried tree leaves that lay scattered about the ground would make under the weight of a
misplaced foot. It was hearing those sounds when the killers came that he depended on to stay alive and, he knew,
for Loraine to have any chance to escape, he had to hear
Nash and his bunch when they came along the trail. He
had to be ready—ready to give up his own life if need be
to save his daughter, to kill as many of the outlaws as he
could before their eyes found him, then their bullets.

Still he wondered about his brother, he knew that Elam
had lived for many years among rough men such as the
ones who sought them. He knew and understood them, and
in many ways he was of the same caliber. He had killed.
Even though Elam didn't talk about it much, Cork knew
he had, and not all under orders from the Army for which
he scouted for ten years. There had been others who had
lost their lives to the gun of Elam Langtry, men who had
absolutely nothing to do with the Army—men who had in
some way broken the simple code that Elam lived by: Don't
try to walk on me, and I won't walk on you. But unlike
the rest of the world, Cork had grown up with his brother
and knew him to be a good man, an honest man, and he
knew without asking that Elam had never killed anyone that
didn't need to be killed. And he also knew that if not for
Elam putting up half the money for the ranch, they would
not have had it in the first place. Yes, even though he never
mentioned it, Elam owned half the ranch and had from day
one, and it was only after Cork took Estelle for his wife
that Elam drug out. Cork had often thought about why his

brother had left but always figured that it was because he and Estelle had married, Elam maybe thinking that two's company and three's a crowd. It wasn't until Estelle died and Elam returned that another notion appeared for the first time. For the first week back, with all the other places for Elam to camp, he camped under the old oak tree where Estelle was buried. Cork would look out from a window or from the barn and Elam would be sitting, talking to her marker, and Cork knew then that his brother had loved his wife and that was the real reason he left. At first the thought angered him; then remembering what a fine and beautiful woman Estelle was, Cork understood how his brother had fallen in love with her. Heck, it was for all the same reasons he had married her himself, but the respect Elam showed for their marriage by walking away and not acting on his feelings showed the true stature of the man Cork knew his brother to be.

A light rustle of leaves suddenly drew his attention. Something was moving along the trail. Cork, sat in the darkness holding his breath, not moving a muscle, straining with every fiber, his eyes, and ears trying to see or hear, but sight was not there and the sound came no more. Once again the trail fell quiet and after a short moment, he relaxed against the rock. He must have dozed off because the next time he opened his eyes he could see, not far, but well enough to know that daylight was not far away. The dark jagged outlines of the trees and boulders around him were starting to emerge from the darkness. He could sure use a hot cup of coffee. Adjusting the shotgun in his lap, he stretched his legs out straight, rubbing at their numbness with a easy hand, and as the circulation returned, the sharp, tingling feeling faded. In a nearby tree an owl hooted and took wing, and to the east a nightingale called out loud to his mate. Down the creek the turkeys he had heard going to roost the evening before were starting to stir and from time to time, he could hear one of the hens chirp. Just the start of another beautiful day, he thought to himself. Then giving his present situation some thought, he wondered how it would end—would it end as it had started, beautiful and peaceful, or would it, sometime before the darkness came again, turn into just a date to be placed on his headstone sitting under that old oak tree? Turning his eyes toward the heavens, he focused on a dimming star. He smiled and gave his head a little nod, and he muttered, "Thanks again, Estelle, for helping me through this long, lonely night." And as if it had heard his words, the little star flickered and was there no more. Cork sat for a while longer letting the light grow brighter, and when it had, he let his eyes move slowly along the trail below and then along the ridge to the east, and when satisfied that all was well, he slowly pushed up to his feet and started toward the wagon. As he broke from the brush, his first sight was that of Loraine; she stood back in the shadows and when she saw him, she smiled and called out, "Good morning, Paw."

He quickly took his finger to his lips and said in a low voice, "Not too loud, Loraine."

"Sorry, Paw." Pointing toward the wagon, she added, "Luke's awake."

"That's good," Cork replied. "If we can only get 'im somewhere where he can rest for a while and stop all this moving around, maybe the boy will start to mend. Have you seen anything of Two Toes?"

"No. Not yet."

"Well, he'll be here before long," Cork replied. Walking in the direction of a cottonwood dead-fall, he said, "I'll gather some wood and start a fire, and while you're fixin' breakfast I'll hook up the litter."

"Okay," Loraine answered with a nod. "I sure could use a cup of coffee."

"We all could," Cork answered. Coming to the wagon, he stopped and looked over the side. "How you feeling?" he asked.

"Been better," Luke answered groggily. "But I can't complain. Loraine said I had fever—said it broke sometime during the night."

"You were pretty hot when we got here last night; there's no doubt about that," Cork replied. Placing his hand on the sick man's forehead, he added, "Yeah, that's much better .... Well, anyway, we'll have something to eat here in a bit and some hot coffee. Then we'll be moving on up the hill. You hungry?"

Luke gave his head a weak nod. "Yes, sir, I sure am." Cork returned the nod and walked on.

After eating, Cork doused the fire while Loraine started loading one of the buckboard horses with supplies, and to the other team horse they attached the litter and had no more than got that done when Two Toes rode from the brush. "We go now," he said.

"Okay," Cork answered. Gesturing with a hand toward the wagon, he said, "I'd be obliged, Two Toes, if you'd give me a hand loading old Luke there."

The Indian drew up his spotted horse and slid to the ground; then he, with Cork and Loraine helping, took Luke from the back of the buckboard and placed him gently on the travois. With that done, Cork stepped into leather; reaching down, he took Loraine by the hand and pulled her up behind him. With Two Toes leading the horse pulling the sick man and leading the way, they started north.

For the first couple of hours travel was easy, but after crossing a narrow, dry creek bed and working their way through a wide patch of mesquite, the grade got much steeper. Coming to a rocky ridge, where trees growing thick and tangled formed an unpassable barrier, Two Toes swung his horse west and rode parallel to the blockage for over a mile. Coming to a narrow break in the rocks, he turned his horse through it, into a little horseshoe-shaped meadow covered in a rich green stand of buffalo grass. Crossing to the far side, he rode up on a spring running shallow with cool, clear water. There, he drew up and slid to the ground. "Rest now," he said. In the shade of a towering pecan, he dropped to his belly and dranked.

Cork, after helping Loraine to the ground, swung his leg over the saddle, and stepped down himself.

She walked straight to the litter to check on Luke.

Cork turned his eyes south checking their back trail, turning back, he asked, "How much further?"

"Not far," Two Toes replied. "We will be there before the moon comes two times."

"Two days!" Cork answered. "Why, I can ride over this mountain from one side to the other easy in two days."

"Maybe," the Indian replied coldly. "But not pulling a sick man, or without leaving a trail for others to follow." He paused, then added, "Maybe too far—maybe you go back to wagon. Take girl and sick man with you."

"No, no," Cork answered, seeing his words had stung hard at the ears of the old Indian. "It's not too far—I understand, and I'm obliged to you for taking us in. I'm just tired that's all, Two Toes—I wish it was over." Taking the canteens from the saddle, Cork walked to the spring and filled them. After a short rest they mounted and made their way slowly on north. A short time later they rode upon a rocky cliff, and at its wind-swept edge they drew up. From there they could see for miles in either direction and not more than a hundred and fifty yards downhill Cork cast his eyes upon the winding trail they had used to get here.

Two Toes slid from his horse. "Walk from here," he said, pointing to an eyebrow of a trail clinging narrowly to the cliff face. Motioning with a hand for Loraine to come closer, he handed her the lead rope to the horse pulling the travois and said, "You lead this one." Turning, he started along the trail.

"Loraine," Cork called out. "You be careful."

She nodded her head in reply and took to the trail behind the spotted horse.

For the first fifty yards all went well. All of a sudden the trail rose a mite, then broke away sharply for about twenty yard or so, and at the bottom it narrowed to no more than three feet wide making it narrower than the rails on the travois. At that point Cork took the rope from his saddle and with one end tied Luke securely to the litter. Placing the other end around the outside rail of the travois, he took it up and tied it off to the harness hame giving the rail some support. Looking at Loraine, he said, "You bring my horse and the pack horse and I'll lead this one."

The horse balked, but Cork pulled on the lead rope, and the horse, seeing the spotted horse take to the trail, cautiously started his feet. The inside rail of the travois rubbed hard against the wall of the cliff and the outer rail hung off the side, touching nothing but air. Luke moaned at the roughness of the ride, while holding on as best he could. The horse, walking on nervous feet, made his way along the narrow trail thirty yards or so to a place where it widened to fifteen feet. There, Two Toes handed Cork his reins. Taking up a double hand full of prairie grass, he walked back up the trail and brushed out the tracks. With that done, he returned to his horse, climbed back into the saddle, and led the way on north.

During the day, they changed directions several times, once even backtracking over their trail. Twice, Two Toes had ridden from the trail in the opposite direction, breaking small limbs on trees as he went, laying a false trail for the pursuers to follow. Near dark they rode upon a small, grassy flat, dotted thick with tall cottonwood, and it was backed on the west side by a sheer ridge of rock some twenty feet high. At half that distance, a spring seeped steadily from a crack, trickling into a nice little pool at the bottom.

"Make camp here," Two Toes said, swinging to the ground.

Cork wasted no time in stripping the saddle and pack from the tired horses. Next, he drove pins, staking the animals on grass, and while he was doing that, Loraine gathered wood and started a small fire. In one pan, she put water to heat so she could bathe Luke's wounds, and after adding coffee to the pot she set it over the flames, and she quickly sliced bacon into a skillet. She knew she needed to get supper over with and the fire out before it got dark to keep anyone—especially Laughlin's men—from seeing its flames, thus pin-pointing their exact location.

With Two Toes' help, Cork unhitched the travois with Luke still lying on it and dragged it over, propping one end up on a boulder. The sick man looked up. "I sure hate I'm causing you folks so much trouble," he said.

"Think nothing of it, Luke," Cork replied. "You'd do the same for me, wouldn't you?" He gave his head a hard shake and added, "Anyway, we've got to get you back on your feet, so we can ride into Rising Star and take the town back from Laughlin and that bunch of outlaws."

Luke smiled and gave a faint nod. "We'll get it back, don't you worry, Cork. If it's the last thing I do, I'm going to kill Maxwell Laughlin if I can. Not only for the good folks of Rising Star, but mainly because he's the one that gave the order to have Paw killed."

"You better watch your step, Luke," Cork replied. "Don't forget they've got them three warrants out for your arrest. That kinda gives 'em the right to shoot you down on sight."

"I'd forgot about that—I've got to talk to Radford and that deputy of his. They know what happened—they were there—but you're right, Cork, gettin' 'em to tell might take some doing. One thing for sure, if they do tell that I killed those McKuens in self-defense, Laughlin will kill them."

"Paw," Loraine called out from the fire, "supper's ready."

"Come on, Two Toes," Cork said. "Let's eat some supper."

As the two men approached, Loraine handed each a plate of food. Taking up another, she walked to where Luke lay. "You ready to eat something?" she asked.

"Not a minute too soon," Luke replied. "I'm about to starve. I can rub my belly and feel my backbone."

"After you eat, Luke," Loraine said with a smile, "I'll clean up your wounds and change the bandages. Tomorrow sometime we should get to Two Toes' camp, and you can rest without all this moving around; maybe you'll start to mend." She brushed some dead leaves from the top of a rock with her apron and took a seat. After cutting the meat she forked it and put it to his mouth.

At that instant, Luke looked into her eyes—those beautiful, dark brown eyes that over the years always seemed to have a reason to sparkle. It was then he realized that he was not looking into the eyes of a little girl anymore but a full-grown woman—a woman he had loved for as long as he could remember—and whose memory had been with him each day since he had left. But knowing she looked at him only in the light of a brother, he figured it best not to make his feelings known. Then early one morning, he packed up and rode from the little town of Rising Star, leaving behind his paw, and he thought, the feelings he had for Loraine Langtry, but the latter proved to be impossible. He knew, too, that it was not right for him to be thinking any such way because soon, if Laughlin or one of his men didn't kill him, he would be gone back up north to his job. And with his paw dead, he didn't figure on ever coming back to Texas. Still he looked, taking in all her beauty, fully aware of his thoughts and strange feelings. He felt the sudden urge to touch her, to hold her, to tell her how he felt. But he somehow fought off the overwhelming temptation and remained silent, knowing that if death didn't find him, he would soon be gone again, taking with him only the memories.

"You need a shave," Loraine said suddenly, breaking the silence.

He reached up, rubbing at the thick growth of whiskers along his jaw. "Are you volunteering?" he asked. Jerking his head toward his old saddle, he added, "If you are, there's a razor and strap over yonder in my saddlebags."

She smiled and replied, "Maybe—maybe not. What's in it for me?"

"Oh, I don't know," he answered. "What do you think it's worth?"

"I'll do it on one condition," she said with a girlish giggle.

"What's that?"

She paused for a long moment, then said, "You have to promise me, Luke, that when you get well, and we get back home, that we'll go riding like we use to—down by the creek."

The statement for a moment left him short of words, but after giving it some thought, he said, "I'll do that even if you don't give me a shave."

Her eyes brightened. Pushing up to her feet, she walked toward where his saddle lay. After giving him a hard-fought and sometimes painful shave, she bathed his wounds and changed the bandages. "There you go," she said. "All done."

"Thank you, Loraine," he replied. "There for a minute I didn't know if I was going to survive or not."

"It's not my fault your beard's so coarse—and you know, Luke Ludd, that old razor there ain't the sharpest in the world. You're lucky I didn't use it to cut your throat just to shut you up. The way you were squealing and caring on."

He laughed. "That did sound pretty bad, didn't it?" Looking up, he said, "Thank you, Loraine."

She smiled back. "You're more than welcome, Mr. Ludd. Now you get some rest and I'll see you in the morning, but don't forget, Luke, you owe me."

"I won't—and thanks again. Good night."

On her return to the fire, her paw stood and kicked dirt on the flames. "Did you get Luke taken care of?" he asked. Reaching, he took up his shotgun.

"Yes, I did," she answered. "Where's Two Toes?"

"He's out there somewhere—he walked from camp a bit

ago. I better get on my way too, before it gets too dark to see where I'm going."

"Okay, Paw, you be careful. I'll get these plates cleaned up, then I'm going to turn in."

"All right, Loraine. See you in the morning; maybe your Uncle Elam will be here by then."

"I hope so; I'm sure worried 'bout 'im, Paw."

"No need to worry 'bout 'im, Loraine. He's been in a whole lot worse scraps than this before. He'll be along; I just don't know what's taking 'im so long." As he walked from the camp, his image faded into the early evening shadows.

"I hope you're right, Paw," Loraine said under her breath. Picking up the dirty plates she gave them a wash and crawled into bed.

Daylight found Cork making his way back toward camp from where he'd spent the night watching the trail. He rubbed lazily at the week's growth of silver-gray stubble along his jaw. *She ain't offered to give me a shave,* he thought to himself. Then shaking his head he mumbled, "She could do a lot worse than Luke Ludd." He had not made it to within sight of the camp when he heard the action on a Winchester slide. His pulse quickened at the sound, and his heart raced as he dropped to the ground beside a tree. Slowly, he let his eyes move along the nearby ridge but the search reveled nothing. He started to call out to warn Loraine so she could run, but stopped when he heard the words, "You're getting too old for this." Recognizing the voice he smiled, but he stayed down hoping to see his brother before he moved. After a moment, he gave up and said, "Where are you?"

"Sittin' in front of this tree here. You're looking right at me."

Cork, looked more closely, focusing on what he thought to be a rock, then he saw movement. "Dammit, Elam, how do you do that?"

As Elam stood up from his hiding place and started off down the hill, he heard a twig snap; he jerked his head to see Two Toes standing looking back at him. "I thought I left you over on that hill yonder watching my horses?"

"You no fool me," the Indian said, "I saw you come up the hill, and watched while you made camp, then saw you go—followed you here."

Elam shook his head and replied, "Like I said, I'm getting too old for this."

"How did things go back home?" Cork asked.

"I'll tell you 'bout it after we've had some coffee."

"Sounds like a good plan to me," Cork replied, and with him leading the way, the three men walked on toward camp.

"Uncle Elam," Loraine called out, seeing the men break out of the brush. Standing up from the fire where she had just moments before started a pot of coffee, she ran and jumped, throwing her arms around his neck she gave him a hug. "I've been so worried 'bout you."

"Well, now. That's something different. I've never had anyone to worry 'bout me," he replied. "But you better let go now, girl, you're messing my hair and wrinkling my shirt. You haven't forgot how to make coffee, have you?"

"No, I haven't," she answered. Turning back toward the fire, she said, "Well, come on. Come on over by the fire and I'll get you a cup—you can see for yourself."

"I'll sure take you up on that, Loraine." Looking to Two Toes, he said, "That's my niece there—she was worried 'bout me."

"You make much noise when you walk," Two Toes answered. "Maybe she should worry." Turning, he started from camp.

"Hey!" Cork shouted. "Where you going? Don't you want some coffee?"

"No—too hot," he answered. Pointing, he said, "After the old man's horses."

"Who you calling an old man?" Elam called out, but not getting an answer, he turned back to the fire and said with a smile, "That old Indian's pretty slick—he had me. I'm just glad he wasn't huntin' hair. If he had been, mine would be hanging on his lodge pole right now."

Cork glanced up from his coffee. "Yeah, he's slick all right—got the drop on me down by the wagon. Never heard or saw nothing until I felt that gun barrel in my back. By the way, how did you find us here?"

"Well, you were leaving a trail a blind man could follow," Elam answered, then after a short pause said, "No, y'all did a pretty good job covering up your trail, but I saw where the litter rubbed against the side of that cliff, and it didn't take me long to figure out the back tracking and the two false trails. I did a little work on all of that, but still not enough to fool Nash. I haven't seen anything of 'em since I left your place. They did shoot my dun horse though, right after I killed Benson."

"You killed Heath Benson?" Cork looked up, surprised.

"Yep, shot 'im right in the head. I was looking to kill Nash, but he didn't show. He was across the way 'bout halfway up the ridge, east of the house. After I shot Benson, Nash took a shot at me blind, that's when he hit the horse. I led 'em south and when I noticed the horse was hit and leaving a blood trail I got down and let 'im go. I don't know how far he went before he stopped. He may still be going for all I know. The man that was with the other two

men I killed the morning before came back with 'em—
Benson killed him—I don't know why for sure, but I heard
Benson tell Barton after he shot 'im that he was a coward
and that Laughlin wanted him dead. And old Sadie killed
another man that I'd never seen before—tore his leg right
off, then ripped his guts out."

"I knew she had it in her," Cork broke in. "I'll have to
see she gets extra grain for that."

"No," Elam replied. "She didn't make it, Cork—they
shot her."

"Sadie's dead?" Cork questioned. "That was the best
durn sow in these parts—a little mean, but still a good
sow—made me some money over the years, she did. I'll
be hard pressed to find another one like her."

Elam looked over and said, "She almost got me too—
that morning. If not for the other sow's turning over the
feed barrel at just the right time she would have too."

"I'm sure glad she didn't. But that's still bad—her gettin'
killed and all."

"How's Luke doing?" Elam asked. "How's all this traveling going with him?"

"All right, I reckon. He was talking last night, and Loraine gave 'im a shave. If nothing else, if we have to bury
'im he'll look a sight better."

"I heard that, Paw," Loraine said abruptly. "And you
know, he looks just fine with or without a shave."

Elam looked over at his brother. Cork looked back, giving his head a shake and his shoulders a shrug. "Don't look
at me," Cork said. "I don't know what's going on. But since
we're talking 'bout Luke, we better go get that litter hooked
up. Two Toes will be getting back before long, and we
need to be on the trail."

The two men walked from the fire, and while they

hooked up the litter, Loraine picked up around camp and loaded the pack. When Two Toes returned, they ate bacon and bread. When they had finished, Cork put Luke's saddle on Mousy and after helping Loraine up into it, he doused the fire, mounted, and started north.

Two Toes led the way on his spotted horse; Loraine followed, leading the horse pulling the travois. Cork led the pack horse, and rode some distance behind, along the ridge to the west. And Elam—well, didn't anyone know where he was for he had disappeared again, but they knew that even though they couldn't see him he was there—if not right there, not far away.

The morning air was cool as they rode. It blew easy among the branches of the cottonwood, pecan, and oak that grew along the creek, making the leaves dance as it made its way. To the east, the sun shined bright, its rays lay warm upon the land, bringing warmth to the trail and to the bodies of both man and beast.

Not far along the trail, Cork drew up among an outcropping of rocks; he sat gazing south, his eyes searching the hills for movement or a flicker from maybe the sun's rays reflecting off something—a rifle barrel or maybe even a belt buckle. Then letting his eyes move slowly along the skyline, he watched for a puff of smoke or wisp of dust— anything that would let him know that Nash and his band of killers were coming, were closing in. Seeing nothing but what God had put there, he touched the horse with a spur and rode on, but in his heart he knew that sooner or later he would look back and they would be there. Laughlin had given Nash a job, and Cork knew that men of his caliber didn't quit until the job was finished or Nash himself was dead. And if they did get lucky and kill Nash that would still leave Bill Powers, Frank Clancy, and all the rest to deal with.

By midday the grade had gotten much stepper, forcing a slower pace, but coming to several old oak trees that grew from among an outcropping of large boulders, they drew up in the shade to let the horses rest and eat. Climbing back in the saddle, they pushed on, trying desperately to make it to their destination before dark.

Another hour along the trial, Cork rode alongside Two Toes, and asked, "How much further is it to this camp of yours?"

"Not far," the Indian answered. Pointing to a rocky ledge covered thick with scrub cedar three maybe four hundred yards on up the side of the mountain, he said, "There."

Cork gave a nod. Drawing up he waited for Loraine, and when she got to him, he said, "It won't be long now, girl." Throwing up a pointing hand, he added, "Two Toes said the camp's on that ledge yonder." Casting his eyes to the injured man, he asked, "How you making it, Luke?"

"I sure think I'm going to make it, Cork. If I can just somehow manage to hold on and not fall off this moun-tain."

Cork laughed at the comment; then touching the horse with an easy spur, he rode on. For the next couple of hours the going was rough, as they worked their way through one stand of trees after another and down one almost unpass-able, for the travois, narrow path between two rocky ledges. Coming to where the trail fell away to nothing, Two Toes drew up and slid to the ground. Dropping his reins, he walked out onto the wind-swept ledge and stared south. Turning back, he took up his reins and led the spotted horse off into a deep cut that ran along the face of a rocky ledge for about thirty yards, then under the low hanging branches of several massive old oak trees. But breaking out from under them, the trail opened up into a little valley no more than two hundred yards across, and knee-deep in rich green grass. There, he stepped back into the saddle and led the way on across to the far side. Coming to a little stream running deep with cool, clear water, he drew up again, and after sliding to the ground, he said, "Here is camp."

They quickly stripped the riggings from the backs of the tired animals; then making their way across the stream over a bridge made of carefully placed stepping stones, they hung the saddles and harness over the low hanging branches of a tree. With Two Toes leading the way, they walked along a narrow path that led them through a thicket of wild plum trees and, a few yards later, across a gravel bed some thirty yards across. Then along a narrow five-foot-wide path which on the inside was shouldered by a rock wall that stood some fifty feet straight up, and on the outside was nothing but air for the better part of two hundred feet or more straight down. On the far end the path opened up onto a rocky flat. The outer edge was skirted by the line of scrub cedar that Two Toes had pointed to earlier in the day. And they gave no indication to anyone approaching from downhill of what lay behind them. Turning, the old Indian led the way in behind a large boulder to a shelf some thirty yards across and at least that much if not more deep, entirely overhung by the cliff above and completely invisible from all directions.

Cork walked deeper under the overhang. Off to one side, he saw a pile of old blankets that made up a bed, and not far away a pit for the fire. Behind it was a rack loaded with some kind of dried meat, and along the east wall was a fairly good-size stack of firewood. Hearing a trickle, he looked toward the back to see water running steadily from under a rock, across a rocky shelf, and falling off it into a little pool at the bottom.

"What'd you think, Paw?"

Cork jerked his head at the sudden question. "Loraine, if we're not safe here," he said, walking back toward the front, "we're not going to be safe anywhere. But right now we better get the pack unloaded and Luke taken care of."

"I'll help," Two Toes said.

Cork gave a thankful nod and replied, "I'd sure be obliged, Two Toes, if you'd give me a hand carrying Luke." Back out on the flat, he walked over to the line of cedar, and looking between their limbs as best he could, he gazed down the mountain to find that they were no more than two miles, maybe less, from the very spot where they had left the wagon—just two miles—and it had taken the better part of two full days to get here. But he could also see why it was so hard to get anywhere near this place without Two Toes knowing you were coming. From where he now stood, he could see for miles in any direction. He let his eyes move slowly along the sloping mountainside and the trees and broken land to the south—an intense search that started at the furthermost reaches of his sight and worked back getting closer and still closer—looking for any sign of Nash and his men or even Elam for that matter, but after seeing nothing, he turned and started for the horses.

While Loraine unloaded the supplies from the pack, Cork and Two Toes took Luke off the travois and after closing the rails that had been made wide enough to go on either side of the horse to a width a man on each end could carry, they loaded him back on and in no time had him safely within the walls of the cave.

"I will be back," Two Toes said making his way toward the mouth of the cave.

Cork gave his head a nod, then walking to the stack of wood, he gathered up an armful and at the pit started a fire. While he was doing that, Loraine filled a pan and the coffee pot with water from the spring and moments later placed them over the flames. After grinding a few coffee beans between two rocks, she added them to the pot; then turning to her paw she asked, "I wonder if Uncle Elam will be here in time for supper?"

"I can't answer that, Loraine. He—" His words was cut short by Two Toes walking back into the cave.

"Here is good medicine," he said, showing Loraine the bunch of leaves and twigs in his hand. "Mix with water, rub there on rocks, make good medicine. Put on hole in man's body. He be well soon."

Loraine, not really being sure, looked to her paw. He nodded his head okay and said, "Go ahead, Loraine, and do what he said. Add a little water to 'em and work 'em up into a poultice."

Dropping down to one knee, Two Toes dipped up water from the pan into what looked to be an old bean can. To it he added leaves and sat it near the flames to heat. When it had boiled for several minutes, he removed it from the flames and said, "Let cool, then sick man drink—all."

After bathing Luke's wounds with the warm water, Loraine covered them with the thick salve, then handed him the can. Luke drank the liquid. In no time he was sound asleep, and moments later sweat started to seep from the pores of his skin.

Two Toes stood looking down at Luke. "Medicine working," he said with a nod, then walking back to the fire, he dropped crossed legged to the ground.

After supper Cork stood up and walked out onto the flat. The moon and stars hung bright in the dark sky, and a nice little breeze blew cool from the west. Crossing to the cedars, he looked through them, his eyes searching the darkness. *Where's Elam?* he thought to himself. Then he saw it—a sight that made his blood run cold. There about where they'd left the wagon—a flicker from a campfire. Was it Elam, who had for some reason gone back? No, Cork explained to himself, and if it was, he would have never built a fire out in the open where it could be seen.

Chapter Five

It had been a long four days since Cork had seen the flicker from the campfire in the bottom, but as of yet, he had seen no sign of Nash and his men, or anyone else for that matter—not even Elam.

Two Toes seemed to come and go at all hours, never staying in camp for any length of time, usually just long enough to eat a quick bite; then he'd disappear again. And when he was in camp, he never said much and spoke only when someone spoke directly to him.

Even though it had only been four days, Luke seemed to be doing a little better. That awful-smelling salve Two Toes had Loraine mix up and put over Luke's wounds was doing the trick—the drainage from the bullet holes had dried considerably and the feverish-looking redness around them was starting to fade. Whatever it was that Two Toes was forcing Luke to drink made him sweat profusely, and it seemed to make him want to sleep all the time, causing him to have short-lived bouts of delirium at which time he'd called out Loraine's name over and over again.

Cork stood up, and flipping the last few drops of coffee from the cup, he handed it to his daughter. Turning back, he took up his newly cleaned shotgun and walked from the cool shade of the overhang out onto the flat where from the clear blue sky the sun shined bright and its golden rays brought warmth to the hillside. He lazily pushed his hat back; then taking a couple of short steps to his right, he put himself in position to see through the small opening that he had cleared through the thick tangled branches of the cedar. It gave him a good unobstructed view of the sloping, tree-covered mountainside below. To the distant south, he could see the trees standing tall and jagged along the creek where they'd left the wagon. He studied the terrain as far as his eyes could see but saw nothing out of place. He didn't understand why Elam hadn't come into camp yet—had he been captured, or maybe even killed? If he was dead, Cork knew that it wasn't due to a gunshot because if someone had pulled a trigger in either direction for miles, he would have heard it. And the chances of someone slipping up on Elam and putting a blade in him or cutting his throat were slim. On the other hand, Two Toes had made it to within just a few feet the other morning. But knowing his brother, he knew that it was in his character to hang back—not being seen while watching their back trail. Surely, he had seen the campfire in the bottom and would want to be here when the attack took place.

Hearing a sudden high-pitched shriek, Cork turned his eyes toward the heavens to see a hawk starting his dive. Moments later the attack was over and the bird sat on a rocky ledge just a couple hundred yards downhill, with his wings spread out wide over his unsuspecting prey. "When Nash and his men come it'll be just that quick," Cork muttered to himself. *We've got to be ready,* he thought. "Where is Elam?" All of a sudden a strange feeling came over him—the feeling that someone was near and watching. He jerked his head around to find the old Indian standing just a few feet away. "Dammit, Two Toes," he said, throwing up his hands. "You shouldn't be walking up behind a person like that. You're lucky I didn't shoot."

"The noisy one is coming," Two Toes said.

"The noisy one," Cork questioned. "What are you talking about?"

"Your brother," Two Toes answered. "There," he said, pointing. "Along that ridge."

Cork looked in the direction of the Indian's pointing hand. "Where?" he asked. "I don't see anything."

"He'll be riding from behind those trees along the draw—maybe he figures I don't see—but I see. I spot 'im long time ago." He turned and walked slowly back toward the overhang and camp.

For the next couple of hours, Cork watched the hillside closely but never saw the first sign of any movement being made by a man or beast. "That old rascal must be seeing things," he muttered to himself.

"Seen anything?" A voice called out from behind.

Surprised by the sudden voice Cork spun to see his brother walking up with a cup of coffee in each hand. "By gum Elam, I'm glad you're here. Two Toes said he saw you coming. But I was startin' to think he was seein' things. You know, livin' up on this mountain all alone can't be good for a person's eyesight or his mind either for that matter."

"Oh, I don't know, living alone has its advantages,"

Elam replied. "No one to kick and complain, and if you do there's no one there to hear it. And if you happen to get a bur under your blanket, there's no one there to try to get you right before you're ready." Getting to within arm's length, he handed Cork one of the cups. "But anyway, here, I figured you might be ready for some hot coffee. It's mighty fine. Loraine's gettin' to be a top hand at makin' it—good and strong, just the way I like it."

Cork took the cup with a nod, then asked, "You see the fire the other night—down in the bottom?"

"Yeah, I seen it. It was those two McKuen brothers and five other men, none of which I've ever seen before. Don't have any idea who they are or where they come from. Didn't see anything of Nash and his bunch though. Barton and his men rode out the day before yesterday morning headed west. I could have killed two of 'em easy, but not knowing where Nash is, I held up—no need in rushing things; it'll happen soon enough." Looking back toward the overhang, he asked, "How's Luke making it?"

"Old Two Toes had Loraine mix up a concoction made from some leaves and twigs that he brought in, and after she had, she rubbed it on the wounds. Then Two Toes mixed up another batch and got Luke to drink it. It's got one heck of an awful smell to it, but it looks to me like it's doing the boy some good."

"That's good—I'm glad to hear it." Changing the subject, he said, "When they come, Cork, they've got to come right up that trail yonder—that's the only way to get up here. I found a trail on the backside but it ran out at the lip of a rocky cliff back yonder a ways—seventy feet or better straight down. No, sir, if they come and we both know they will, we'll be looking at 'em. Old Barton is leadin' 'em, and it'll take 'im some time to work out all the false trails we've put down but even as stupid as him and Quint are there'll figure 'em out—it'll just take 'em some time. I just hope Nash and his bunch don't hook up with 'em before they do."

"I wonder where Nash is?" Cork asked.

"I don't know," Elam answered. "He may be back in Rising Star with Laughlin, or he may be holding back somewhere letting Barton lead the way in hopes to draw us out into the open. Then him and his bunch will swoop in and finish us off—he's smart, Cork, and he's got smart men ridin' with 'im."

"Let 'em come!" Cork half shouted. "I'm ready. You know, Elam, I've never been one for trouble, but on the other hand I've never been one to run from it either, and I've gone 'bout as far as I'm going. The cards have been dealt, now it's time for Laughlin to call, raise, or fold."

"I agree, Cork. But we need a few more days so maybe Luke will get to feeling better—we could sure use his gun. And I don't know how much of a fighter that old Indian is going to be, but I'm figuring him to be here at the end. If not," he added with a slow worrisome shrug of his shoulders, "so be it. But Nash or anyone else is going to find themselves hard pressed to get across that clearing out yonder without gettin' themselves killed. And if they do somehow manage to make it across they've still got to get from there to here and the only way to do that is to come along that narrow trail with no place to hide. No, sir, we may not get 'em all, but one thing for sure there'll be fewer live ones going down the hill than came up it."

"Y'all come on; the food's ready," Loraine called out.

Elam looked to his brother. "Go on and eat something, Cork; I'll stand guard."

"Ain't you hungry?" Cork asked.

"Yeah, but someone needs to keep watch. You just be sure to let me know when you're finished."

"Okay," Cork replied, turning. He started toward the overhang, but seeing Loraine coming with a plate of hot food, he smiled and asked, "Is that for me?

"It's for whoever's staying, Paw. I kinda figured one of you would stay out here and keep look-out."

"That would be me," Elam replied. "You're spoiling me, girl; I've never had anyone to even care whether or not I eat much less go to the trouble of bringing it to me."

"Well, I guess that just goes to show you how special you are, Uncle Elam."

His face flashed red with embarrassment and his eyes brightened at her comment. "Special—oh no, girl, I wouldn't go that far—to say I'm special or such."

"You are, Uncle Elam," she said with a smile. "You're very special to me and Paw. I don't know how we'd made it without you, and Luke owes you a special thanks too."

When she had walked to within reach, Elam took the plate, then giving his head a thankful nod, he said, "Old Cork there is awful lucky to have a daughter like you—just like your mother, you surely are. But enough of this silly talk, you better get back in there and get your chores taken care of—you probably need to be looking after Luke or something like that." Turning, he looked through the opening, casting his eyes once again back upon the loneliness of the mountainside and under his breath, he said, "How you like that? She thinks her Uncle Elam is kinda special."

Back under the overhang, Luke lay atop a pile of blankets, moaning, and thrashing his arms about, fighting with a bout of delirium. Somewhere along the way, he remembered dozing off or maybe becoming unconscious.

Vaguely, he remembered bathing his face and his fever-cracked lips with cool water—cool water from where? he thought—or had it been someone else who had done the deed for him? He tried hard to remember, but the dull throbbing pain coming from several places on his body and the constant roar from the pounding in his head kept him from thinking clearly. His face and body felt as though they were on fire, and he remembered reaching up and lazily swiping at the heat and some force stopping his hand. Then, he felt something soft and cool touching his brow and all along his face and neck, but not understanding what or why, he lay motionless, afraid he was dying.

A faint wind stirred, and the smell of burning wood filled his nostrils, and from somewhere not far away he heard a trickle of water splashing lightly over rocks. With the passing of time so went the coolness, and slowly the heat returned, but as it did the soft touch of what felt to be someone's fingers moved slowly across his forehead and down along his face—fingers soft, gentle, and cool.

He opened his eyes and looked up to see only the jagged rock overhang above him. The coolness on his face now just a distant memory, but the feel of the soft slow moving fingers moving across his skin remained.

Out of the corner of one eye, he caught a glimpse of something moving. Turning his head a bit sideways, he focused more closely, and upon realizing it was Loraine, he smiled and said, "What are you doing, trying to kill me again? I sure wouldn't doubt it for a minute after that shave you gave me the other day."

Her dark eyes brightened at the sound of his voice. "I'll make you think kill. Luke Ludd, you've had me worried to death with all your senseless blabbing and thrashing around." She pushed her long black hair back from her beautiful face, and asked, "How you feeling?"

"I don't rightly know how to answer that, Loraine. I'm hurtin' all over, but the pain tells me I'm still alive." He sniffed at the air. "What in the world is that awful smell? I hope its not something you're cooking."

"No, its not anything I'm cooking, and, Luke Ludd, you better watch your mouth," she said with a little laugh. "It's a poultice made from some leaves and twigs that Two Toes brought in and showed me how to mix up. That's what I've been putting on your wounds, and he made up a batch of something else and you've been drinking it, but yesterday, he said you'd had enough. So today you haven't had any. I guess maybe that's why you're awake now." After a short pause she asked, "Do you remember getting here? Do you know how long we've been here?"

He slowly shook his head. "Don't have any idea, Loraine. All I remember is it getting awfully rough in a couple of places—how long?"

"Four days," she answered. "And your wounds seem to have healed more in those four days than they had in the three weeks prior to that. You're on the mend now Luke you'll be up and about in a few days."

"I want to thank you, Loraine, for taking care of me. Without you and your paw I don't think I would have ever made it. And, of course, your Uncle Elam and Two Toes had a big hand in it too. I need to thank them all."

"No thanks needed," Cork called out from the fire; standing, he walked toward where Elam stood guard. "Well, it looks like Luke's going to make it. He's in there right now yapping his fool head off and Loraine sitting there giggling at everything he says. I don't know for sure but I think there's something suspicious going on there."

"Kinda looks to me like you might be right, Cork. I got that notion the first time I saw 'em together—that maybe there was something beside doctoring going on, maybe a tidbit of wooing. But you know, Cork, she could do a lot worse than old Luke in there. With the exception of taking on all five of those McKuens at one time, he seems to have a fairly level head on his shoulders."

"She's not old enough to be thinking of such things. Elam she's just a little girl."

"I don't know what Loraine your lookin' at, Cork, but the one I'm seeing is a full-grown woman."

Cork studied his brother's reply for a long moment, then letting out a long, ragged breath, he said, "I hate to admit it, Elam, but you're right. Where has the time gone—the years I mean—seems like it was only yesterday that she was following me around on them little ol' skinny legs of hers, askin' me questions. Like why pigs squealed when they're hungry, and why butterflies were always just out of reach, and why the sun came up just to go down again and where it came from in the first place." He shook his head. "No, sir, I didn't always have the answers, but me and her mammy, God rest her soul, did the best we could."

"I think you and Estelle did one fine job, Cork, and I think you've got a good girl there—one you can really be proud of, and I'm sure when it comes time she'll make the right decisions."

"I hope you're right, but just in case, I'll keep an eye on her. You know she don't need to be thinking the way she is if Luke's going back up north after this thing is over."

"That's right too. If he's not going to be stayin' on, he sure needs to let her know before this thing gets out of hand. Tell you what I'll do—you keep an eye on her, and I'll keep an eye on him. How does that sound?"

"I'd be obliged, Elam. I don't want to see her heart broken if I can help it. And she'd get awful mad if she knew I was buttin' in or even thinking about it."

"Okay, then," Elam replied. "Why don't you go try to get some sleep, so we can change out around midnight? Right now we've got more important things to worry about. If Nash and his bunch get up here, we won't need to worry about Loraine and Luke or anything else for that matter; we'll all be dead."

"Oh, I'm not really worried. I just want her to be happy, but you're right; we've got a meaner horse to ride right now."

Elam watched his brother go; then turning his eyes back upon the mountainside, he watched the trail with a careful eye while he ate at his plate of beans.

Roscoe Nash sat alone at a little table in the back of Red's saloon tossing down a shot of rye. He sat awaiting word from Frank or Bill that they had found the men they sought or at least found someone who had seen them. He watched the door as he had for the previous two days, with the fading expectations of seeing Luke or maybe one or both of those Langtrys or maybe all three walk in. But as time passed, he knew that it was he himself who had made the mistake. The men he so badly needed to find and kill had not come to Caster, and he was slowly realizing it. But the trail he followed led right to the outskirts of town—not so much the tracks made by the horse hooves, but the blood trail left by the wounded horse, and there in the deep sand, among some wagon tracks and footprints left behind by bare feet, the blood had stopped and the trail had mysteriously disappeared. He had never in all his life been tricked by a false trail but the more he thought about this one, the more it seemed that this time that's exactly what had happened, and that more than anything angered him. Underestimating the ability of an adversary was not something he did, or he hadn't up till now, but that was nothing that couldn't be rectified as soon as he found them—and he would find them. It was just a matter of time, and when he did, he would kill them and he knew, the sooner the better.

Bill Powers pushed his way through the batwing doors with Frank Clancy and four more men trailing behind. Stepping quickly across the plank floor to where Nash sat, he drug out a chair and dropped down. Frank took a seat across from him, and the other men took a seat at the next table over. "Seen anything?" Bill asked looking to Nash.

"No, I ain't seen nothing. If I had they'd be dead bodies laying here and there. Look around Bill do you see any dead bodies?"

"They're not here," Clancy cut in. "We've looked under every rock in this one-horse town and talked to half the people—ain't nobody seen 'em."

Nash shook his head. "No, they're not here. I've done figured that out. That's why you haven't seen 'em; they went north. That old tracker put down a false trail and, acting like a young fool on my first job, I followed it—it had to be him—I don't think the pappy or even Luke Ludd is that smart. He killed Benson, too, that old bastard did, and I bet somewhere between the house and there where the trail turns to come here, he got off that bleeding horse and circled back—and to make matters even worse, we left those three horses at the house saddled." He paused, then giving his head a hard disgusted shake, he called out, "Barkeep, bring us a bottle."

"What do you want to do now?" Frank asked.

"We're going after 'em, that's what we're going to do," Roscoe growled. "Who knows—Barton, Quint, and that bunch of idiots riding with 'em might have already found 'em. For all we know Luke Ludd and that whole bunch is already dead, but I doubt that very seriously—that old man's smart—too smart for the likes of Barton and Quint McKuen. But who knows?" he said with a light shrug of his shoulders. "They might just get lucky. When I suggested they go north I didn't know I was puttin' 'em on their trail. I was sendin' 'em north just to get 'em out of our hair. Anyway, we'll ride back to Rising Star and check with Laughlin. If we don't find Barton there with him, we'll ride back out to the house and see if we can pick up the trail from there."

Frank jerked his head toward the next table, then speaking in a low voice he asked, "You want to take those four over there with us—or leave 'em here?"

Nash, slowly poured a drink from the bottle; then he filled the other two glasses. "Might as well take 'em," he answered in a whisper. "There's nothing they can do here, and, who knows, we may need someone to put out front to lead the way, no need in us taking any big chances when we've got them to do it for us."

"Here, here," Frank said, raising his glass high. "That's what I like about you, Roscoe; you're always thinking of everybody's welfare."

The three men sat silent for the better part of an hour, sipping at their drinks; all of a sudden Roscoe said, "You know, when we get Luke Ludd and Cork Langtry taken care of, that will give Laughlin what he wants—full rein of all the water in the whole valley and control of Rising Star and all the land for miles around it. I've been thinking how would you boys feel about settling down—about maybe puttin' down some roots. What if I could talk Laughlin into making me a full partner on this deal?"

"How is Laughlin making you a partner going to help me and Frank?" Bill asked.

Roscoe smiled. "Well, if me and him were partners and something happened to him—say he somehow came up with a bad case of lead poison and died . . ."

Frank looked over at Bill Powers and smiled and Bill smiled back, "Ohhhhh, I see what you're getting at," Bill replied. "And being the only partner left alive, you'd have to do your duty and take over."

Roscoe looked up, "Uh-huh, and we'd have that whole town right where we want 'em—eatin' out of our hands." He adjusted himself in the seat; then leaning on an elbow, he looked across and said, "Heck, I could be the mayor and you and old Clancy there could be the law. That would mean gettin' rid of Leroy Radford and that deputy of his, but Laughlin's wantin' them dead anyway, and the good part is he's already paid me for seeing it gets done. And every one that was in the Driftwood the other day heard Laughlin and Leroy fightin'—it would be easy enough to make the townfolk believe they killed each other."

"How you going to get it done?" Frank asked. "What makes you think that Laughlin will make you his partner?"

"I ain't got it all worked out just yet," Roscoe admitted. "That's the part I'm still working on. But if we don't find Luke and that bunch and get 'em dead, it won't work anyway." Draining the last few drops from the glass, he sat it down on the table, then sliding his chair back, he got to his feet. "Let's ride," he said. Then motioning to the four men sitting at the next table, he called out, "Okay, men, toss 'em down and let's get out of here."

A short time later, amidst long shadows and the dying

glow of the sitting sun, Roscoe led the group from the livery stable. They made their way slowly along the wide dirt street, and at the crossroads, they swung toward Rising Star and kicked their horses into a canter. They rode east with the sun fading fast behind them. Coming to where the trail of the bleeding horse had played out, Roscoe threw up a hand bringing the group to a sudden stop. There in the dim light, he cast his eyes to the deep sand and the few tracks that still remained, and as he eased his horse forward to have a closer look, he cursed at the thought of being bettered—being made a fool of. And he made himself a promise that it would never happen again—that Elam Langtry had seen his finest hour. And the only way to get the bad taste of defeat out of his mouth was to find Elam Langtry and kill him and all of those who rode with him.

Disgusted, he spun his horse, but when he did, he caught a slight glimpse of something moving. There, along a distant ridge in the dimness of the late evening skyline, he saw a wagon. Standing tall in the saddle, he look closer. "Well, looky there, men. I think we just found who we're looking for."

"What are we waiting for?" Clancy called out. "Lets go get 'em. I'm ready to get this deal over with."

"That ain't them," Bill replied. "Y'all know they'd never travel out in the open like that. They're too smart to do something as half-witted as that."

Roscoe jerked his head around. "You're probably right, Bill, but let's go have a look anyway just to make sure. Who knows? It might be them, thinking that by traveling out in the open we might not waste our time coming to check. But I know one thing; if it is them they've out smarted themselves this time."

They rode spread wide through the mesquite and prickly

pear in the direction of the slow moving wagon, and as they drew near it became obvious that two men sat on the seat and another rode in the back. And then they saw something that made their pulse quicken. One of the two horses tied to the back was a zebra dun, and he was favoring a leg.

"That's them," Frank half shouted. "That's the horse, the one Roscoe shot. See 'im limpin'?" Reaching, he slid the Winchester from its boot and worked the lever, making sure there was a bullet in the chamber; then he lowered it letting the stock come to rest on his leg.

Seeing the group of men ride cautiously toward them, the man driving the wagon reached under the seat and took up his own rifle and after feeding a bullet into its chamber, lowered it to lay across his lap. "'Evening," he called out in a cold, hard, voice. "What can I do fer you gents?"

"Get your hand away from that there gun is the first thing you can do, old-timer," Roscoe answered. "That's if you want to keep on livin'."

"Don't mean any harm," the man said, moving his hand away. "You fellows came up on us so fast, it kinda gave me a start. My name is Potee—Jess Potee—and this here is my boy Clem. That there in the back is my son-in-law William; he's married to my daughter Ruth."

"I don't give a damn about any of that," Roscoe shouted. "What I want to know is where you got that horse—that dun there—the one that's limping?" Touching his horse with a hard spur, Roscoe rode around to have a better look, and sure enough there it was—a hole in his right shoulder.

The old man chewed nervously at his lip. "We didn't steal 'im, if that's what you're thinking. We found that horse, yes sirree bob; we sure did, found 'im three, maybe four days back standin' in among some trees half dead maybe three miles from this very spot, back yonder way," he said, throwing up a hand toward the south. "He wasn't wearing no saddle or nothing like that and he was hurting so bad he didn't want to move so he was easy to catch. We looked around a mite, but didn't see anyone live or dead that he might belong to, so we took 'im. We've been over to Prat Creek to see my brother, his wife and family. Old William back there patched 'im up and got the blood stopped. But if'n he belongs to you, then by God you can sure have 'im back, and of course, there won't be any charge for the doctoring."

"Don't have any need for the horse," Roscoe replied. "But I'd like to find the man who left Rising Star riding 'im. You wouldn't happen to know a Luke Ludd or Elam Langtry would you?"

The old man shook his head. "No, sir, can't say that I do, but I can't talk for the other two here. How 'bout it boys, you heard of 'em?"

"No, Paw," the one on the seat beside him answered.

The one in the back didn't speak; he just shook his head no.

"If I find out you're lying to me, old man," Roscoe sneered, "I'll kill you—I'll kill you and both these boys here. Now wouldn't that be a shame, to die over something like that. Now if you know where Luke Ludd is, you better tell us."

The old man's tone softened and he spoke with a shaky voice. "Don't know any Luke Ludd. I swear, mister, I don't know 'em. We found that horse like I said, and that's all I know. If I knew any more, I'd sure tell you."

Rascoe gave his head a hard nod. "You better be right," he said. Jerking his horse's head around, he put a hard spur to his sides and rode off.

The old man wasted no time in starting the wagon.

Clancy touched his horse into a canter and rode up alongside Roscoe. "You think we should follow 'em?"

"No," Roscoe replied, "that old man didn't know anything. Didn't you see the fear in his eyes? If he'd known, he'd have told us. No, sir, Luke and that bunch went north; of that I'd bet a man all that I have." Swinging their horses back onto the trail, they headed east, but they had not gone far before darkness fell upon the trail, and they rode on through the night without speaking, making their way along the dark, dusty trail as nothing more than seven unrecognizable shadows. At daylight they drew up to let the horses rest and to build a fire for coffee. A short time later they pitched the saddles back on, and after dousing the fire, they stepped back into leather and rode, tired and hungry, toward Rising Star.

Just as the sun settled on the west horizon, they rode into the little town, and after making their way along the wide dirt street to the Driftwood, Roscoe drew up and stepped to the ground. Handing his reins to one of the four lesser men that rode with them, he said, "Take 'im on to the livery. Rub 'im down good and make sure he gets extra grain." Motioning with a hand, he said, "Frank, you and Bill let 'em take your horses and put 'em away, and we'll go in here and see if we can find something to eat and maybe a little something to wash this trail dust out of our throats." Tossing a silver dollar to each of the four men, he added, "When y'all get those horses taken care of, ease on down to the Ann Mayre and get yourself a drink, and if you see Barton McKuen or any of his bunch come let me know." He hitched his pants and adjusted his gunbelt, then leading the way through the batwing doors, they found a table in the far back near the door leading into Laughlin's office and took a seat.

"Flo, what have you got back there to eat," Roscoe asked the dark-haired waitress walking up.

"I don't think there's anything left, Mr. Nash. We did have some beans earlier, but I'm sure they're all gone by now." She paused to think. "Do you want me to send someone over to the café to get you something?" Turning toward the bar, she called out to the bartender, "Hank, do we have anything left back there to eat?"

"The beans are all gone," Hank answered. "But I think there's still some sandwiches back there."

"Sandwiches will be fine," Roscoe said, looking up. "Bring 'em and bring us a bottle of your best whiskey."

The three men ate what she brought and sat for the next hour sipping their drinks; then the door to Laughlin's office opened and they looked over to see Leroy Radford walking out. He looked up, and upon noticing them, he immediately spun on his heels and disappeared back into the room closing the door behind him.

"What do you make of that?" Bill asked.

"Come on and we'll go find out," Roscoe replied getting slowly to his feet. At the door, he pushed it open without knocking and walked in. His eyes quickly scanned the room. Behind his desk Laughlin sat fumbling at some papers and looked up surprised. Leroy Radford stood by the window, looking down at the street below, but at the sound of the door opening, he turned, and headed out, having to turn sideways to squeeze between Roscoe and the door facing. "Hey Leroy, what's the big hurry?" Roscoe asked.

"No hurry," Leroy answered without looking up or slowing down. "It's just time for me to be checking the doors, making sure everything is locked up."

Roscoe, watched him go, turning to Laughlin, he asked, "What's wrong with Leroy? He looks like he's scared to death."

Laughlin shook his head and gave his shoulders a shrug. "Hey I don't know what's wrong with 'im—he's been acting a mite strange the last couple of days—the one big thing is he's a coward." Gesturing toward a chair, he said, "Roscoe, have a seat—Bill, Frank, have a seat." Pointing, he added, "There's a bottle; help yourself if you want something to drink."

Bill Powers nodded a thank you; then taking up the bottle, he filled a glass.

"Did y'all get Luke and those Langtrys took care of?" Laughlin asked.

"Not yet," Roscoe answered. "But we will; you need not worry about that."

"Oh, I'm not worried. But I need it done, Roscoe, and the sooner the better. I can't get a deed to that Ludd place out there until I can prove that Luke has abandoned it or that he's dead. And we both know he ain't just going to drag out—no, we've got to kill 'im. And if he's already dead, we've got to produce his body."

"Well, if you asked me," Roscoe cut in, "I don't believe him to be dead, but I do think he got shot and that he's wounded—how bad I have no idea." He shook his head. "I don't know what it is that makes me think he's still alive. I've not seen any hard evidence pointing one way or the other, it's just a gut feeling I have."

"You're not scared, are you, Roscoe?" Laughlin asked with a meaningless chuckle. "The thought of Luke Ludd maybe still being alive don't scare you, does it?"

The killer's eyes narrowed and his lips grew instantly thin, and in one motion, he pushed up from his seat and his left arm swiped the desk clean of all that sat upon it. His right dropped for his side-arm and in a flash, he had the hammer thumbed back and the muzzle within an inch of Laughlin's already pale forehead. "You looking to get yourself killed, Laughlin?" he shouted. "Do I look scared—huh? Maybe I should put a bullet right between those miserable eyes of yours just to show you how scared I am."

"Now, now, there's no need of all of that, Roscoe," Laughlin choked out. "I know you're not scared. C'mon fellers, I was just talking."

"Well, since we're just talking, me and the boys here think that maybe since we're going to have to do so much killin' to get you clear of this deal, that the pay should be a little better—maybe a whole lot better."

"I understand. Why didn't you just say something, Roscoe? Why, boys, there's no need in all this gunplay. What do you want—five hundred? A thousand? Two thousand more? Just name it."

"Go ahead and shoot 'im," Frank said in a loud voice. "And we can have it all."

At the last words, Laughlin's breath caught and his body tensed up. Unable to speak, he just shook his head no.

"Now, now, Frank, there's no need in gettin' greedy," Roscoe said. "There's plenty to go around. I was thinking more like half." Pushing the gun barrel right up against Laughlin's head, he asked, "Don't you need a partner in this deal. Not just someone to do the killing but a full time partner. One that will be here long after the killing is done?"

Before the last word fell from Roscoe's mouth, Laughlin was nodding his head yes and a powerless smile had come to his lips. "I was just today thinking about that very thing, Roscoe—about taking you in as a partner."

"I just bet you were," Roscoe roared with a laugh. "But whether you was wantin' one or not you've got one, and it would be to your benefit to like it."

"Okay, Roscoe, that's fine with me as long as we both understand who's the boss and when we take over, the town will be named Maxwell."

"Laughlin . . . Laughlin," Roscoe repeated, shaking his head. "I don't give a hoot what you name this town. I don't care if it's got a name or not. Call it Foolsville for all I care, but as of this minute make no mistake who's running this outfit. Let me put it to you like this, Laughlin; see, it's kinda like you told old Radford. You're at the top because I let you be at the top and you live because I let you live, and when I feel that you're no longer needed I'll kill you and won't think twice about it. Do you understand?"

"Yes," Laughlin mumbled.

"What? I didn't hear you."

"Yes! I understand," he shouted.

"Now what I want you to do," Roscoe continued, "is in the morning, I want some papers drawn up showing that you and me are full partners—fifty-fifty—and that I own half of everything, including the bank, livery stable, general store, both saloons, and of course, half of all the land. When you get that done we'll sign it, and me and the boys here will go take care of Luke Ludd and the Langtrys."

Laughlin looked defeated. "Okay, Roscoe. I'll get the papers ready, and we'll sign 'em in the morning over at the bank."

The killer smiled and holstered his gun; turning, he led the other two men out the door, letting it stand open behind him.

Maxwell Laughlin sat unable to move for a long moment; then standing, he made his way on wobbly, weak legs to the door and closed it, and on his way back, he stopped and picked up the things that lay scattered about the floor and placed them back on his desk. In shaky hands, he took up the whiskey bottle; nervously, he pulled the cork and filled a glass; taking it up, he tossed it down. But with his thirst not nearly satisfied, he took up the bottle again and turned it up taking three or four big gulps. Walking to the window, he looked down onto the street while trying to think of a way out. He knew he could never take Roscoe in a fair fight, or Frank or Bill either for that matter. No, he needed help and he needed it fast. Maybe someone like Max Bear from Longview or Sam Perkins from Dallas, both top gunfighters, but getting either one of them would take time and that was something he didn't believe he had.

Crossing to the door he pulled it open and stepped out, but had not taken more than a couple of steps when he spotted the man he was looking for, and when the sheriff looked up Laughlin called out, "Come in here." Turning, he walked back into his office, and he had no more than dropped back to his chair when Radford walked in.

"What can I do for you, Mr. Laughlin?"

"It's Roscoe—he's taking over. You've got to do something, Radford; you're the sheriff. He said he was going to kill me. I want him arrested. And Frank Clancy and Bill Powers is in on it too."

"Laughlin, have you lost your mind? I'm not going to buck Roscoe Nash. You did this yourself, Maxwell—you brought 'em here and now you've made 'em mad, and if any of us get out of this thing alive, it will surprise me."

"You can't just let 'em shoot me down in cold blood, Radford. You've got to do something; you're the law in this town, dammit! Hey, wait a minute—Barton—yeah that's it. I want you to go find Barton and tell 'im I need to see 'im."

"Maxwell, I can't find Barton. Where would I look? He may be dead. Did Roscoe say anything about 'im."

"No, he didn't. And now that you mention it, I wonder why Barton and Quint wasn't with 'im?"

"I regret ever gettin' mixed up in this deal, Maxwell. And I hate that I ever let you talk me into trying to kill Luke Ludd in the first place and filing those bogus murder charges on 'im. If he ain't dead—you don't only have Roscoe and that bunch to deal with, which God knows is enough, but you got Luke coming after you too." He reached up and ripped the badge from his shirt; pitching it down on the desk, he said, "Here you can have this, I'll have no more to do with it; turning on his heels, he started for the door.

Laughlin drew his gun and thumbed back the hammer. "Hold up, Radford," he said. "Don't make me kill you."

Radford spun. "Go ahead, Laughlin—shoot. Looks to me like you're going to need all the practice you can get. But you can't kill me, because I died a long time ago, the day I met you."

Laughlin tightened his finger on the trigger, but as Radford turned to walk out, he relaxed it. Right now, he had more to worry about than Leroy Radford, and Leroy was nothing he couldn't take care of himself later. Right now, he had to figure out a way to get word to Max Bear and Sam Perkins and anyone else that would come. He needed some fast guns and he needed them yesterday, but he had to do it in a way that Roscoe wouldn't find out until it was too late. In the morning, he would draw up the papers and he and Roscoe would sign them. Afterwards Roscoe would leave town going after Luke and Cork Langtry. Then and only then would he be able to send a wire, and depending on how long it took Roscoe to find and kill Luke and get back to town, that was exactly how long he had to get the two new men here. On the other hand that time might be better spent gathering up what he had in cash and lighting a shuck himself. "No," he mumbled, "I've worked too hard and too long to just give up now." Taking some paper from the desk drawer, he started preparing the paper they would sign, giving Roscoe half of everything he owned.

The next morning, after reading the paper carefully, Roscoe Nash signed his name and Maxwell Laughlin signed his. "Now don't you feel better having a partner, one that will look after your interest and one that can protect you?" Roscoe asked.

"Yes, I do," Laughlin answered. "Now get out there and find Ludd and those Langtrys so we can get this deal finished up."

Roscoe put out his hand and Laughlin took it. "I think this is going to be a long and very profitable partnership, Laughlin, but to see that you don't go and do anything you'll be sorry for later, I'm going to leave Bill here to watch after you."

"No need in doing that," Laughlin said. "I can manage, and you might need 'im."

"I'd just feel better knowing that he's here with you." Letting go of Laughlin's hand, Roscoe turned and walked out the door. At the hitch-rail, he whispered something to Bill Powers; then stepping up to leather, he led the group slowly out of town knowing he was a very wealthy man, and with Laughlin sooner or later out of the way, he would even be wealthier.

Bill stood and watched them go. Walking back into the

bank, he took a seat at the desk across from the man he had been left behind to watch.

Laughlin cleared his throat and after a moment, he said, "Powers, there's no need in you hanging around here. I'll be okay, and Roscoe, well, he might need you."

"He sure might, and before he gets back he might wish I was with 'im, but he told me to stay, Laughlin, and that's what I'll be doing until I hear otherwise." Gesturing to a stack of papers laying on the desk, he added, "Now you just go on and do whatever it is you need to be doing and don't fret yourself none over me."

Laughlin gave his head a worried nod and wiped the nervous sweat from his brow with the back of his shaky hand. He knew Bill Powers had not been left behind to protect him but to make sure he stayed in line and to kill him if he crossed that line. *What am I going to do now?* he thought to himself. *I need to get to the telegraph office. I need to send a wire.*

Chapter Six

It had been a long day and even a longer night for Maxwell Laughlin. And in that period of time, he had not been left alone for one second; he could not so much as go to the outhouse without Bill Powers tagging along. The killer had stayed all day at the bank, sitting, watching and watching even closer if someone happened to get within Laughlin's reach. And they had eaten supper together over at the café, and now Laughlin lay in his bed and from time to time, he could hear the plank floor just outside the door in the hall squeak when Bill would adjust himself in the chair in which he sat watching the door or when he'd get up to move around trying to restore the circulation in his legs.

Surely, he would need to sleep before long, and Laughlin could make his move then. He needed to get to the telegraph office where he could send the wire, or get to where he'd be able to pass a note telling a friend to send the wire for him. But that would be even harder than trying to get

120

there himself, for he knew that in this town he had no friends and anyone he gave the note too might just hand it over to Bill Powers.

But there was Flo, the dark-haired girl who worked in the saloon. Laughlin had used her services several times over the years and had paid her well. He quickly glanced at the pillow where many a night she had laid her head, and at that moment, he realized for the first time, that in this world, he was all alone—with no friends and no one to care.

Flo would be his best shot, but he needed to have the note ready, and he knew it needed to be small enough that he could conceal it in the palm of his hand, keeping it from the view of Bill Powers' watchful eyes. He raised to a elbow and gazed through the darkness to where he knew the writing table to be. He tried to envision all that lay between where he now lay and the table where he'd find a pencil and paper. He could not risk lighting a lamp, for Bill would see its glare through the gap under the door, and bumping into something that would make a noise would surely bring his captor running. No, if he went, he couldn't afford to make any mistakes; his steps would have to be silent, and he had to be very careful not to bump into anything getting there, and he'd have to be just as careful getting back.

He slowly threw the covers back and rolled swinging his legs over the side of the bed as he pushed up to a sitting position. He sat for a long moment, listening, watching the gap under the door for any sign of a shadow that would tell him that Bill had heard something and was standing with his ear to the door. Then, he slid slowly off the side letting his feet come in contact with the rug covered floor. Hearing a loud pounding noise, he stopped, but realizing it was coming from within his own chest, he pushed up to his feet. Slowly, he turned, and placing one foot carefully ahead of the other, he started the long journey. Ever so slowly, he moved silently through the darkness with his hands leading the way, constantly moving, searching the darkness for any unremembered object that might stand in his way. All of a sudden his hand touched something and he instantly stood frozen. Had he come far enough for it to be the writing table? He didn't think he had but in a place where sight was useless, and distance could not be measured in any other way, he was not at all sure. Inching closer, and still closer, he nervously let his hands come in contact with the object before him, slowly letting them work their way along its outline, they shaped what he thought to be the table; then feeling the back of his chair he was sure. Slowly, he reached down, and ever so quietly slid the drawer open just enough to get his hand in and take out what he needed. Then running his hand cautiously over the top, he found a pencil and by the coal oil lamp a few matches. Having all he needed, he turned and headed back for the bed and had taken only two steps when he heard Bill shuffle to his feet. Thinking for sure the killer was going to open the door, Laughlin lengthen his stride and in doing so misjudged where he thought the bed to be and kicked the leg of the iron bedstead with his bare toes, bringing to his whole body an instant wave of pain. He bit hard at his lip trying to stifle a grunt or groan and leaped for the bed, just barely getting the covers pulled over him before Bill opened the door and stuck his head in, but he did not speak.

Laughlin lay with his eyes closed, and a short time later, he heard a squeak and then a thud as the door closed. After giving Bill time to get settled back in his chair, Laughlin sat up in the bed and leaving the cover draped over his head, he struck one of the matches and began to write.

Flo,

I will pay you five hundred dollars to send these wires. One to Max Bear Longview, Texas. The other to Sam Perkins Dallas, Texas. Tell them to come quick. Ten thousand dollars for each. Flo, be sure not to tell anyone about this.
Laughlin

With his note finished, he folded it tight and tucked it neatly inside the bib of his long johns, then placing the pencil and burnt matchsticks deep inside his pillowcase, he rolled over and closed his eyes, but sleep would not come. Every time he started to doze off, he saw a muzzle flash and Bill Powers smiling.

The next morning the first thing Laughlin saw when he opened the door was Bill Powers sitting in a chair leaning back on two legs asleep, but at the sound of the door opening, his eyes shot open. "Where do you think you're going?" he asked.

"I'm going to work," Laughlin replied. "But first I want some coffee. You hungry?"

"No, I ain't really hungry, but I sure could use some coffee."

"Well, come on, I bet old Hank can fix us up."

"Hank!" Bill questioned. "What's wrong with the café?"

"Well, if we just want coffee we can get it downstairs in the saloon, and it won't be so crowded. But if you want to go across to the café, then let's go."

"Oh, now that you mention it," Bill replied. "I don't

guess there's any need. We can drink coffee downstairs if you want too. It's all the same to me."

Shoulder to shoulder they made their way along the hall. At the bottom of the stairs they crossed to a table and took a seat. Near the front, four older gents sat at a table by the window playing a game of dominos, and in the far back old Ted, the town drunk, sat still asleep, slumped over the table where he'd passed out and spent the night.

"What will it be, gents?" Flo asked with a big smile.

Laughlin smiled back and slapped at his leg. "Come here and have a seat," he said. "Where you been keepin' your pretty self? You haven't been up to see me lately."

She stepped around the table and dropped down to his knee. "I was thinking about coming up to see you last night, but some cowboy came in," she said with a giggle. "And it's not all my fault, Maxwell, you told me never to come up unless you sent for me."

"I know, but it would sure be nice if you'd come by and surprise me ever once in a while." As he talked, he was working his hand ever so slowly around to her dress pocket, and when he had found it, he dropped the note inside. Then giving her a good firm slap on the bottom, he asked, "Flo, do you know Mr. Bill Powers?"

"Why, yes I do," she answered. "I had the pleasure of his company one evening not too long ago. And I know Roscoe and Clancy too." Looking over she gave a smile and said, "Good morning, Mr. Powers."

"Bring me some coffee," Bill growled, rubbing at his tired, bloodshot eyes. "I didn't come in here to talk to any whore. So shut up and go get us some coffee."

Her body tightened at the man's harsh words, but she didn't reply. Instead she stood up slowly from Laughlin's knee and as she walked off, she said, "Two cups of coffee coming right up."

After drinking their second and third cup, Laughlin drew his watch from his pocket and gave it a quick glance. Standing, he said, "We better go. It's time to open the bank." Pitching two bits down on the table, they walked out and crossed the street to the bank.

Like the day before, Powers sat watching as Laughlin talked to customers and went on with his work of taking care of bank business. And from time to time Laughlin would look over to find Bill had dozed off, but never for long. That night again they ate supper in the café; later in his office, Laughlin worked on some papers, but before going up to the room, he and Powers stopped by the bar to have a drink. They had just ordered a third drink when Laughlin looked up to see Flo coming down the stairs on the arm of some cowboy. When their eyes met, she looked nervously to Powers and when she was sure he wasn't looking, she nodded her head yes to Laughlin, letting him know she had sent the wires.

A long sigh escaped Laughlin's lips. Turning up the glass, he tossed it down. "You 'bout ready?" he asked, looking over at Powers.

"As long as you're buying I could stay in here all night," he answered.

"Good evening, Maxwell," Flo said, walking up. "How 'bout it—you want some company?"

"No," Powers answered abruptly. "He don't want any company."

She stood with her hands on her hips, staring down at Laughlin for a long moment, then asked, "What's wrong, Maxwell, is Powers talking for you now?"

"No. He ain't talking for me," Laughlin replied. "But I

am tired, so I guess I'll pass, maybe tomorrow night, Flo." Laughlin reached taking the wallet from his inside coat pocket. "Here," he said. "this should hold you." Taking out some money, he pitched it down on the table.

She picked it up and smiled. "Thank you," she said, sticking it down deep into her bodice. Turning away, she walked to the bar and started talking to some rough-looking stranger.

"Laughlin," Bill blurted, "you just gave that floozy five hundred dollars. Hell, you can buy fifty women with that kind of money."

"I don't know," Laughlin answered with a unknowing look on his face. "Was it that much? I didn't count it."

"I think I better get you on up to your room. Roscoe wouldn't like it—you throwing your money away like that."

"Roscoe can go straight to the devil," Laughlin snapped defiantly. "Like you said, Powers, it's my money and I'll do with it as I please." Pushing up quickly from the table, he led the way toward the stairs.

Powers laughed. "The way it was told to me, Laughlin, two hundred and fifty of that money you just gave to that whore belonged to Roscoe."

Laughlin spun, his mouth twisted, and his fist clinched white.

"Hold on, Laughlin," Powers said with a chucking laugh. "Remember that gun you're packing ain't got no bullets in it. But since you've gone and done what you did, I'm going to tell you something that I don't want you to ever forget— and that is, if you ever spin on me again, fill your hand because I'm going to kill you. I'm going to shoot you graveyard dead." After a short pause, Bill Powers, gestured toward the stairs with his hand, and added, "Now if you know what's good for you, you'll turn around and go on up to your room."

After preparing for bed, Laughlin blew out the lamp and crawled in. He lay for a long while in the darkness, looking over from time to time in the direction of the door when he'd hear Powers out in the hall moving about—wondering when he'd burst through the door and carry out on his threat. *But if he's going to kill me he better do it,* Laughlin thought, *and he better do it soon, because in a few days I'll have a big surprise for 'im. One I don't think him or any of the rest is going to like. I've got to stay alive just a few more days—just a few more days, and I'll have some help.*

Cork stood guard in among the cedar, his weary, blood-shot eyes watching the mountainside, his mind exhausted from the eight days he had done nothing but what he was doing now, and his nerves thin from the waiting and the uncertainty of what today would bring.

When they come will it be just Barton, Quint and the five men that Elam had seen at the campfire, or will there be more—will they have Nash and his bunch of no-telling how many riding with them? Will they try to come up the hill in the daylight or wait until night and try to make good their assault under the cover of darkness, their way being lit only by the glow of the moon and stars—or will there even be a moon? To these questions he had no answers. He would have to wait and when it happened, he would have to react quickly and accordingly.

Hearing a light grunt and the shuffle of feet over rocks, he spun, but seeing who it was, he smiled. "How you feeling this morning?" he asked.

"Almost like new," Luke answered, standing propped on

a crutch made from a mesquite root. "Thought I'd come spell you for a while. I think Loraine's got some food cooked up in there. You hungry?"

"Not too awful hungry, but I could sure use some coffee."

"Well, I'd say you're in luck; she's got a big pot made and it's mighty fine, had two cups myself, and she's got some bacon and beans cooked up too."

"Well, then, if you think you can watch the hill, I'll go see what she's got." Looking up he asked, "I see you've had a shave. Loraine been shavin' on your face again?"

"No, I did it myself," Luke answered. "I even walked off down to the creek and took a bath."

Cork gave a nod. "You must be feeling better. It's been good seeing you up and about the last few days. You're awful lucky, Luke—lucky to be alive." Throwing up a hand, he added, "I think I'll go on in and see what Loraine's got cooked up."

"Yes I am, Cork," Luke replied to the man's first statement. "Take your time, I've got this covered out here." When Cork had gone, Luke dropped to a rock and sat looking through the small clearing. At times he worked his arms high above his head trying to lessen some of the tightness. He would flex the fingers on both hands repeatedly, but he worked mostly with the fingers on his right hand—his gun hand. They needed to be loose and flexible. He sat looking through the cedars at the roughness of the mountainside. He had never realized until just a few days ago how beautiful this country really was and how close he'd come to not ever seeing it again. Two of these people who had put their own lives on the line to save his, he had known all his life, but he had not realized the strength of their character until now.

Cork had been his father's best friend. He and Luther Ludd had moved to this country about the same time, and Luke had heard his father tell stories about Cork and how they had helped each other over the years, working the cattle, cutting firewood, building a barn, and a time or two, in the early years, they had even fought Indians and outlaws together. But that for the most part had all happened before Luke was born, and it had not been until Cork pulled him from under the barbershop that Luke had seen the man's real character, and it was then, he understood how Cork Langtry had become his father's best friend.

And there was Loraine, the little girl with her long, black hair done up in pigtails—so skinny and frail, yet meaner than all get-out. He could not count the times, she had kicked him on the leg for something and called out she never wanted to see him again. But every morning, he rode his old horse up to her house, and after pulling her up behind him, they rode off to school—with her arms wrapped tightly around him, and her ear pressed firmly to his back. But all of that had mysteriously changed, and for some reason, he looked at her much differently now. The feelings he had for Loraine Langtry were more than a man should feel for his sister—a whole lot more.

Luke knew Elam Langtry only by reputation, and much of it he'd heard from drifting cowhands sitting around campfires, at bars, and gambling tables across the north. Stories of an army scout and Indian fighter, lightning quick with either fist in a fight or with a gun and relentless once on the trail of a man or any group of men he sought.

Two Toes was another story; he knew nothing of him really. He hadn't known for sure if he really existed until now. He had heard of a club-footed Indian living up on this mountain, but he had never talked to anyone who had actually seen him. And for the most part Luke had grown up thinking it was no more than a story. But here he was as big as life—not happy over white men being on his mountain—but a man with enough heart and understanding to let them stay. But Luke knew that now that he was getting better, the day was growing near that Two Toes would ask them to leave, for the old Indian had no fight with Maxwell Laughlin or Roscoe Nash or anyone else for that matter, and being so far along in the autumn of his life, he wanted none.

At the sound of footsteps, Luke turned to see Elam coming toward him. "Seen anything?" he asked, walking up.

Luke shook his head. "No, nothing that don't belong."

Elam nodded. "That's good. How 'bout you—you feel up to a fight?"

"If it comes, I'll do what I can, Elam. That's all any of us can do. But while we're talking, I do want to thank you for your help and I'm obliged to you for bringing Mousy along."

"No thanks needed; I'm glad it worked out." Looking around to see if anyone else was near and not seeing another soul anywhere, Elam turned back and said, "Loraine tells me you're a Pinkerton man."

Luke nodded. "Yep, that's what I am all right, and have been for six years. I left Rising Star seven years ago after hooking on with a cattle drive going to Abilene. A few days after I got there, I saw a poster saying the Pinkerton Agency was needin' help, so I hooked up with them and I've been there ever since. I work mostly guarding gold shipments along the Union Pacific line."

"So, I guess you'll be going back up north when you're finished here?"

Luke studied Elam's face carefully. Knowing that in this

land of men coming and going, it was kinda their way not to ask questions such as, where've you been—where you going—or what have you done. But realizing who it was asking the question, he thought little of it and asked, "Why?"

"Oh nothing special. I've just kinda noticed that Loraine's awful smitten with you, and I sure wouldn't want to see her hurt. If you feel like you've got to go back, then I understand, but it might be in everyone's best interest to let her know before it gets out of hand."

Luke shook his head. "I'd never do anything to hurt Loraine. I hope you know that, Elam. I'd just never do it."

"It was something I thought needed to be said," Elam replied calmly. "Now it's been said and I'll not mention it again." He stood for a while longer and with no more words, he turned and walked back toward the overhang.

The night came and went without incident, and the morning started out much in the same fashion, but half way through the morning meal Two Toes appeared from out of nowhere and pointing southwest, he said, "They come."

Cork dropped his plate, then grabbing up his shotgun, he headed for the cedars. Suddenly, he stopped and turned back. "Loraine," he called out. "You get back yonder in the corner and don't come out until the shootin' stops."

"No, Paw, I ain't going to do it. Y'all will need someone to load your guns. If you won't let me shoot, then that's the least I can do."

"Okay," he half shouted. Turning, he walked on toward the cedars where Luke and Elam already stood. "See 'em?" he asked.

"Not yet," Luke answered. "They're still too far west. Two Toes said they were riding slow still looking for sign, they're not sure we're up here yet. Maybe they'll ride on by again."

"I'm not looking for 'em to give up this time," Elam explained. "They've already found the opening through the ridge. They had to be this side of it for Two Toes to see 'em coming from the west." Suddenly pointing, he said, "There they are. The other side of those rocks yonder."

"Yep, I see 'im," Cork replied. "Who is it? Can you tell?"

"Not sure," Elam answered. "But it looks like that big bay horse that Barton McKuen rides."

Luke nodded. "That's who it is all right, and there's the rest of 'em coming through that stand of trees just west of 'im."

"Okay," Elam mumbled. "This is it, men. Y'all know what we've got to do—so let's take our places; remember to wait until they start across that clearing out there, then open up. But remember, too, to take your time and make every shot count." Looking to his niece, he said, "Loraine, you get down in behind that rock over there, and when we pitch you a gun, you reload it." But seeing the fear in her eyes, he pulled her close and said, "No need in frettin', Loraine, you're safe here; those old boys don't know it yet, but they've got a long row to hoe before they get to us."

She gave her head a worried but understanding nod. Turning she threw her arms around her father's neck and gave him a hug. "I love you, Paw," she said in a low loving voice. Then looking over at Luke, she smiled and with a nod to him, she added, "You be careful, too."

Cork leaned his shotgun against a rock in easy reach, knowing it would be no good at long range. Taking up his Winchester, he slid the action on it, then he cast his eyes back toward the men in the bottom.

Barton led the way, with Quint second but a little further downhill. And behind him, the other five men rode spread wide through the trees and the coolness of the morning, unaware they had already been spotted, and they rode along looking for sign, totally unaware of the danger that awaited them.

All of a sudden Barton drew up on his horse and sat studying the trail—seconds passed. Turning in the saddle, he called out to Quint and when his brother looked up, he waved him over. The two sat talking for a long moment and when the other men got there, Barton said something to them, but after a bit they swung their horses and rode back west—in the direction they had come from.

"They know we're here," Elam called out in a low voice. Raising his rifle, he took aim and pulled the trigger. The gun's loud roar was followed by a short lived wisp of white smoke and a second later the bullet made contact and one of the men tumbled from his horse, but it was neither Barton or Quint.

"My God, what a fine shot, and downhill too," Luke said, looking over. "That had to be at least six hundred yards or better."

"Just luck," Elam admitted. "I shot into the bunch hoping to hit something, and as luck would have it, I did. It's better than nothing and now there's only six left that we have to concern ourselves with."

The guns at the bottom returned fire, as the men rode at full speed into an outcropping of rocks, but at that distance the lead was hitting the ground way short, not even close enough to force the men at the top to take cover. Moments later the gunfire faded into the early morning, and a horrible quiet fell upon the mountainside.

The wounded man momentarily staggered to his feet,

only to take a couple of steps before collapsing again in a thick patch of mesquite, but this time he would stay down, for he lay dead.

The attack hadn't gone as Elam had planned, he would have liked for them to have been closer—at least to the clearing, so they'd have had a better chance to lessen the number, but the way it had come about, he was lucky to have killed the one. Now it would be a waiting game, one that would consume time—time they didn't really have. Each passing minute was a minute that might bring Roscoe and his bunch, and if that happened, the men at the top would still have a slight advantage over the men at the bottom, but in sheer numbers it would be less of an advantage, and one that might shift the other way quickly. With that thought in mind, Elam let his eyes slowly search the mountainside for a way down, knowing he needed to get close enough to get off a clear shot. But he realized, he would have to cross the same clearing he had planned to trap Barton and his men in coming up, so he decided to stay where he was and give the men at the bottom time to make the first move.

By midday, the sun shined bright and hot from high in the cloudless pale blue sky, and right over where the dead man's body lay among the rocks and twisted mesquite, one lone buzzard circled wide, sometimes swinging in low to have a closer look, but still cautious of the men hunkering in the rocks nearby.

Elam adjusted his rifle in one hand and swiped the sweat from his brow with the other. Turning to his brother, he said, "It wouldn't surprise me if they waited until dark before trying anything."

"If they're coming," Cork replied, "I wish they'd come on; this waitin' is 'bout to get the better of me." Just then a bullet ripped at a rock no more than twenty yards down-hill, and the sound of thundering horse hooves filled the air. "Here they come," he shouted dropping down behind cover.

"Just hold your fire," Elam called out. "Let 'em get well within range. I'll take the first one. Cork, you take the second. And Luke, you take the third; then we'll worry about the rest. No need in us all shootin' at the same one." Bringing his rifle up, he sighted down the barrel in the direction of the sound of the horses coming, but when they broke from the brush there was only three and none had a rider, only empty saddles. Knowing he had fallen for an old Apache trick, Elam jumped to his feet, looking west just in time to see Barton and Quint leading the way riding one horse double, breaking north heading for the rocky ledge on which Elam himself now stood. Behind them two more horses followed and both of them also labored under the weight of two men. He raised his gun and pulled the trigger in hopes of another lucky shot, but it was not to be, for this time the bullet went wide and fell harmlessly to the ground. Now with Barton and his men out of sight and within a mere hundred and fifty yards the situation had changed, but Elam knew as did Cork and Luke that for the killers to get to where they needed to be, they were still going to have to cross the clearing and it was there, they would hopefully have their trouble.

Once again a dead quiet fell upon the mountainside, and moments later something no one expected—a gunshot. And a short time later, an unfamiliar voice called out, "They shot Naller."

"Did anybody see where it came from?" another loud voice asked.

"Up there," the first voice replied. "Somewhere in among those rocks."

Elam chuckled under his breath. "That fool old Indian," he mumbled, then looking in the direction of Cork and Luke, he said, "Two Toes got one."

"There he goes," the first voice called out. "Up there, along the—" But before he could finish, the gun roared again and his voice, too, fell silent.

"He got two of 'em," Elam started, but his words could not be heard over the sudden onslaught of gunfire coming from the rocks where Two Toes had Barton and his bunch penned down, but as the gunfire faded, Elam looked over with a smile and said, "Three down and just four to go."

His words brought smiles to the faces of the other two men, and Luke commented, "Things are looking up." But then, his attention was drawn southeast by a distant flicker and the sight of what he saw pushed the smile from his lips, and a worried look quickly washed over his face. "There comes more trouble," he said throwing up a pointing hand.

Elam looked in that direction to see a big, thick cloud of dust rising high above the trees. Not knowing for sure but figuring it to be Nash and his bunch, he said, "It was never a question of if they would come, but more of when—and if we'd have Barton and his bunch taken care of before they did. Now we know, and there's nothing left for us to do, men, but to get ready. And as you can see we ain't got much time—three, maybe four hours before they get here. Maybe a little longer if we're lucky."

To the west a rifle fired, moments later it fired again, but this time there were no voices and no return gunfire. Elam wondered at the silence; had Two Toes somehow managed to kill them all, or were they working their way along the ridge coming this way and keeping their guns quiet, afraid a shot might give away their position, or had they maybe seen the cloud of dust and decided to stay put until reinforcements arrived? The next thought made his blood run cold; had one of them got a shot at the old Indian and killed him?

"Elam," Luke called out from across the way. "You and Cork stay here and watch the clearing. I'm going to work my way around and see if I can get a shot."

"You might oughta think about staying put, Luke," Elam replied. "You're not gettin' around on that bum leg too good as it is."

"My leg's fine," Luke answered, turning to walk away, but stopped at the sound of horses galloping over rocks. Looking past Elam, he saw Barton and Quint riding hard from among the rocks headed in a southerly direction at a full run. Jerking his rifle up, he took aim and pulled the trigger. At the same instant Cork, and Elam both fired their guns, too. Barton leading the way swayed in the saddle grabbing at the pommel with both hands. But Quint, riding some distance behind and feeling the effects of two bullets entering his body, immediately threw up his hands and tumbled from his horse and was dead by the time he hit the ground. Quickly working another bullet into the chamber all three men took aim and fired again, this time at Barton just as his horse left a ledge and disappeared down into a wash. But when the horse came out on the far side the saddle was empty.

"By God," Luke hollered, "we got 'em all. Yes sir, we sure did, we got every last one." Looking over at Cork, he added, "Those last two were the main ones 'cause they killed paw. Now if I can just get Laughlin it'll all be over with."

"Gettin' Laughlin might not be so easy to do, Luke," Cork said, gesturing with a hand toward the ever-nearing cloud of dust. "We've still got to get by them first. Barton and that bunch were just a bunch of beginners compared to what those boys are going to try to throw at us—no sir, it's not over by a long shot. And I hate to say it, but the worst is yet to come."

"Well," Elam cut in, "no need worryin' over it. I'm sure they've already heard the shootin' and from the looks of things, Roscoe's bringing a whole swarm of men with 'im." Looking over, he said, "Pitch me some shells, Loraine, so I can load my gun." Turning back, he shook his head and mumbled, "Oh, Lord, I'm gettin' too old for this."

With the passing of time, the cloud of dust grew near from the south, and Elam knew that it would not be long now before Roscoe would find the wagon sitting along the creek and then the break in the ridge. There, he would find the tracks left behind by the horses of Barton and his men. Elam also knew Roscoe to be smart and very unpredictable, and he knew that a man with Roscoe's experience in tracking down and killing as many men as he had over the years would not approach out in the open as the inexperienced Barton had done, but slower and with much more caution, staying well within the cover of trees. Maybe just sending one or maybe two men beyond that last line of brush out there in hopes they would draw gunfire and in doing so would pin-point the exact location of the men he sought. Then, he would carefully scout the mountain, maybe taking days to do so, looking for the best way to descend upon his prey. And at the end of his careful study he would know, as Elam already knew, that the only way was across the clearing.

"I don't like it," a voice called out.

Elam spun at the sound of the man's voice to see Two Toes walking from the overhang. "You don't like what?" he asked.

"More men come," Two Toes said, throwing up a pointing hand. "You see?"

"Yeah, we see 'em," Elam answered. "And we're obliged to you for helping us out a while ago."

"No big problem," Two Toes replied. "White men easy to find and kill, make mistakes—make much noise, like you."

Elam looked over at the other two men and gave a smile. "Now that's when you know you've seen your better days—when old Indians start talkin' that way 'bout you, and you're glad he's here to said it."

Cork gave a nod, then pointing toward the bottom, he said, "Look there, they've found the wagon."

Elam gazed south just as the group of men drew up in the trees where the wagon had been left. "It won't be long now," he said. Casting his eyes toward the heavens, he noticed that the one lone buzzard that had been before had now been joined by several more. "Death for some," he muttered under his breath, "brings life to others." Then looking upon the faces of each person there, he wondered who if any, would go down the hill as they had come up it and which ones would be left behind, their bodies no more than food for the hungry coyotes and buzzards.

Chapter Seven

From behind the cedars, Elam, Cork, and Luke watched as Roscoe led the group of men from the wagon at a canter due north—straight toward them. They worked their way quickly through the stands of trees and around boulders and the great patches of prickly pear until they reached the point where Roscoe could tell the rock ridge was impassable. There, he drew up on his horse, and sat with his hands resting on the pommel, his eyes carefully searching the mountainside for clues—trying to see anything that would reveal that they were closing in on the men they sought. After giving the mountainside a, long, cautious study, he swung his horse west, and led his band of killers off in that direction, and moments later they disappeared into a stand of oak.

"It may be morning before we see 'em again," Elam said. "How many you figure, Luke, ten—maybe fifteen?"

"I don't rightly know, Elam," Luke answered. "But yeah I'd guess, somewhere along in there."

"I didn't get a count," Cork cut in. "Still too far away, but it looks to me like if half 'em went home, there'd still be a plenty."

"It don't really matter how many there are," Elam said. "They've all got one thing in common; they've ever last one got to cross that clearing out there to get to us. There's no other way unless they climb up that damn cliff back yonder and I don't see 'em doing that. But if they tried, they'd need a rope or something tied off at the top before they could start, or they'd have to have a mighty long ladder. No, we don't have to worry about anything except them trying to get across that clearing." He stood, then turning he started toward the overhang.

"Where you going, Uncle Elam?" Loraine asked.

"I think I'll go see if I can rustle me up some grub, might even have a cup of coffee." Turning back he said, "You boys might want to think about doing the same thing; we may be in for a long night."

"Go ahead," Cork said to Luke. "I'll stay out here and keep watch; y'all try to get some rest too. If'n I see anything I'll give a holler." He stood and watched them go; then turning back, he cast his eyes back upon the mountainside and the loneliness of the day. From the corner of his eye, he caught a glimpse of something move. Standing straight, he looked closer to see a pack of coyotes working their way cautiously through the rocks and brush toward the bodies of the dead men. On the western horizon, the sun hung low, and above its slowly dying reddish orange glare, dark clouds were building looking as though it might rain, but he knew, that at this time of year the chances of that were unlikely. From the top of a tree not far downhill an owl hooted, and on a high up limb of another a buzzard sat with his wings spread wide. From all directions and as far as the eye could see it was peaceful and quiet, but Cork knew that it would not stay this way, for sooner or later Roscoe and his men would return—gunfire would once again fill the air and more bodies would litter the ground. *But that's the only way it can end,* he thought to himself, *when a man like Laughlin tries to take something that's not his and the man he's taking it from don't want to give it up. I could have done it like the Arnetts and Redwines and just sold out to him, and me and Loraine could have took what little he was offering and gone somewhere and started over—no, we couldn't have,* he thought—*my beloved Estelle is buried on that place. If Laughlin gets it, he'll have to do it the same way he got Luther's place—he'll have to leave me lying dead.* A few hours later the sun was gone and a blanket of hazy darkness had settled over the mountainside.

Hearing footsteps, Cork looked in that direction to see Luke making his way from the overhang. "Figured I better come spell you off," he said, walking up. "You seen anything?"

"No, I haven't. And in another half hour it'll be too damn dark to see my hand waving in front of my face."

"You better go on in, Cork, and get a bite," Luke said, motioning back toward the overhang. "Loraine's got some mighty fine rabbit stew made in there, and a big skillet of pone bread."

"Sounds good," Cork replied, walking off, but seeing his brother coming toward him, he drew up to wait.

"Okay, Cork," Elam started. "As we all know, this is where it gets tricky—mighty tricky. We can't see who or

what is crossing or trying to cross that clearing out there—
we can't see nothing in this darkness, but on the other hand
neither can Roscoe and his men. So here's what I want you
to do. I want you to stay in there with Loraine and if
shootin' starts, you douse the fire and y'all get back in that
far corner like we talked about, and if you hear anything
moving around the entrance, open up with that damn
scatter-gun of yours. Me and Luke are going to mosey on
down toward that bottleneck, there where the trail crosses
that gravel bed." Pausing to think, he turned and said,
"Luke, come over here, you need to hear this, too." Turning
back to his brother, he added. "We won't figure on being
back until first light, but if we do for some reason happen
to come back sooner, we'll stop there about that big rock
and one of us will say 'flour sack,' and you answer 'empty,'
If we don't hear 'empty,' we'll know its not you and come
in ashootin'. Luke, the same goes for you too. If you say
'flour sack,' I'll answer 'empty,' or vice versa and remember not to say it in a way that a person might pin-point
your whereabouts and get a shot at the sound of your voice.
Cork, when you get back in there be sure to explain what
we're doing to Loraine so she'll know what to do in case
something happens to you."

"I will," Cork answered.

With the plan laid out, Elam swung his rifle over his
shoulder and with him leading the way, he and Luke started
from the flat along the trail leading north toward the creek.
They moved slowly through the stillness of the night, their
breathing light, and their footsteps silent upon the wind-
swept rock, sometimes having to make their way only by
feel in the darkness, letting a hand move along the rock
wall where in places no moonlight shined at all. Coming
to where the trail widened, Elam knew that it was ten paces

from where he now stood to the old oak tree where he'd
have to duck to go under its low hanging limbs and another
sixteen paces from there to the edge of the gravel bed
which was another twenty-two steps wide. He moved on
and after taking the tenth step, he reached out his hand and
there was the limb. Taking Luke by the hand, he guided it
to the limb, so he, too, would know it was there. Sixteen
steps later he felt the gravel crunch under his feet, and
eleven steps after that, he directed Luke to a rock just off
the trail a little way. "You stay here," Elam said in a low
voice. "I'm going on toward the creek another ten yards or
so. If you hear anything moving over that gravel don't wait
to see who or what it is, just let loose with both them guns
you've got."

"Okay," Luke whispered.

Elam turned and counted his steps back to the trail and
continued on along it to a spot where he could hear the
water barely trickling over the rocks in the creek. There he
turned and walked from the trail with a hand extended in
front of him, searching the darkness for the tree he knew
was there. Moments later his hand came in contact with
the giant old cottonwood. Not able to see, he dropped to
the ground, then laying his rifle across his lap, he leaned
his back against the tree trunk and settled in—waiting—
listening for the sound of a foot maybe slipping off one of
the stepping stones and splashing in the water when someone tried to cross the creek or someone grunting at the pain
the sharp thorns of the plum trees would cause or maybe
the distinctive shuffling of boots walking on the gravel.
Blinded by the darkness, he had only his ears to alert him
to anything coming or going—but that was nothing new,
for he had spent much of his scouting life tracking in the
darkness—looking for an Indian or band of Indians that

traveled only by night, with only the glow of the moon and stars to light their way. With the fading of the moon's dim glow so went the trail of the Indians not to be found again until the moon once more hung in the dark sky. A flutter high in the tree above him drew his attention, but Elam sat motionless not even looking up. Hearing a low, purring chatter he knew it to be a raccoon and that it was probably just making its way to the ground from its nest hanging somewhere high in the tree. But if there was a nest up there, Elam had not noticed it the other day when he studied the trail—counting the steps between one rock and another and the steps from one tree to the next—drawing out in his mind a picture that would make it possible for him to travel it with some sense of direction even in total darkness.

Picking up the scent of the man, the raccoon jumped from about ten feet up in the tree, landed in a pile of leaves, and scampered away. The cool night air stirred again causing Elam to pull his collar tight to his neck. To the north frogs croaked along the creek, and to the south a pack of coyotes howled and yelped, sometimes simultaneously, at the moon and stars as they ripped and ate at the bodies of the dead men. All that could be heard were sounds that were all too familiar to Elam's ears. He had over the years studied them all and knew what they meant and knew, too, that each sound had its own place and time, and for either to suddenly change meant trouble. He also knew that the horses grazing in the meadow across the creek could play a big hand in this deal too. If Roscoe and his men did somehow happen to get across the clearing and find the break in the wall when they entered, the horses already grazing there would either by smell or sight notice the new horses and start blowing and nickering. Elam wasn't expecting that or anything else to happen tonight, but on the

clean up, those buzzards up there will," he said pointing up.

Cork turned up an eye to see the pale blue morning sky dotted thick with low-flying buzzards—circling wide, but with each pass getting lower—ready to move in on whatever the coyotes left. But for now they circled—waiting for the time the coyotes would move on to shade, and only then would it be safe for them to land.

"Y'all go on in," Cork said. "Loraine will have something cooked up in a little while. Y'all eat and try to get some sleep. I took me a pretty good little nap last night while she watched."

"I've had so much rest my joints are startin' to stiffen," Elam answered. "And I'm not at all hungry, but I'd sure take a cup of that good hot coffee that I'm a-smellin; that's if she's got a plenty." Turning, he and Luke started for the overhang but after getting a whiff of the bacon frying and the smell of bread cooking they decided they had better eat a little something, and after they had eaten, they sat sipping their coffee.

"How you feeling, Luke?" Loraine asked taking his dirty plate.

"Just fine, Loraine. You did a mighty fine job patching me up. I'll forever be in your debt."

"Oh, you don't owe me anything," she answered with a blushing smile. "It's Two Toes you need to be thankin'. He's the one who really done the doctorin'. But don't forget, Luke, you did say you'd take me riding when we got back home."

"I remember," Luke answered with a nod. "I told you we would—and you can count on it, Loraine—before I leave to go back north, me and you will go ridin'—we might even pack a basket and have a picnic there under those two big pecan trees where we hung that swing."

Hearing the words *"back north"* forced the smile from Loraine's beautiful face. She quickly turned away and started rearranging some pots.

"Speaking of Two Toes," Elam cut in. "Has anyone seen 'im?"

"Yeah," Loraine answered. "He was here right after you called Paw out. He got 'im a hand full of bacon and a couple of biscuits and walked out. He had to walk right by you. Y'all didn't see 'im?"

"No," Elam answered, shaking his head. Looking at Luke over what remained of a biscuit, he asked, "How 'bout you—you see 'im?"

Luke shook his head no without speaking; flipping the last few drops of coffee from the cup, he handed it up to Loraine. "Here," he said, "you can take this." Standing, he crossed to his bedroll and dropped down. "I'm going to try to get some sleep," he said, looking back at Elam. "Someone wake me in 'bout two hours."

"Okay," Elam replied; then he added, "Loraine, if you would please ma'am—and don't mind—kinda help your old paw keep an eye on the bottom—if you would, and I might just try to get a little shut-eye too."

"I sure will, Uncle Elam. You and Luke just go on and get some rest, me and Paw will look after things. We've had a little sleep, and I know that you two have been up all night." Wiping her hands on her apron, she started toward the flat.

Elam crossed to his bedroll and laid down, but sleep did not come right away. Instead he lay thinking of the devastated look Luke's comment had left on Loraine's face and at this very moment how bad her heart must be hurting.

But as bad as Elam felt about it, there was nothing he or anyone else could do. Luke had made it very clear that he was not planing on staying around Rising Star when this deal was over, and that's all anyone could ask of him. Now it was up to Loraine to pull herself up and to move on with her life. "But can she," he mumbled to himself. Pulling his hat down over his eyes to block the campfire's bright glare, he dozed off.

"Uncle Elam," a soft voice called out. "Wake up, Uncle Elam, they're coming."

He opened his eyes to see Loraine standing over him. Realizing what she had said, he threw back the blanket and scrambled to his feet. "Where are they—how far out—how long have I been asleep?"

"I don't know I didn't see 'em, Paw did, and he told me to come fetch you. You've been asleep 'bout five hours, I reckon."

"Luke," Elam called out. "They're here." Grabbing up his Winchester, he worked the lever feeding a bullet into the chamber and started for the flat. The moment had finally arrived—the moment they all knew would surely come— the moment that would decide who would live and who would die—who would walk down the hill and go home and who would be left behind for the coyotes and buzzards to fight over.

Luke pushed his fingers through his hair and slapped on his old hat. Reaching, he took up his gun belt and swung it around his hips.

"Luke," Loraine said as he worked at fastening the buckle. "You be careful."

He gave her a nod, and turned for the flat. But as he did, he heard, "I love you, Luke." Surprised by the words, he spun on his heels to face Loraine. "What did you say?" he asked.

She bit nervously at her lip. "I said, I love you, Luke Ludd. And I do, Luke, with all my heart. I always have. No matter what happens today—no matter how it ends. I love you and always will."

"I know you do Loraine, and I love you too."

"No," she replied. "It's not like you think, Luke. I don't love you as a brother. I love you as a man, and I always have, Luke. I just thought I'd let you know before you went out there."

He stood for a moment shocked at the news, but not knowing exactly what to say or even how to answer, he turned and made his way quickly toward the flat to where Cork and Elam already stood staring through the cedar, and when he got there, he asked, "Where are they?"

"They're just sitting down there looking this way," Elam reported. "They won't come all at one time—no, they won't; Roscoe's too smart for that; he's already noticed the clearing and figures it to be dangerous." After a pause to think, he added. "Oh, he might move on up to that next line of trees out there. It wouldn't surprise me if he did that, but he won't come any futher. From there he'll probably just send one or maybe two men to see if they draw gunfire. When he does, we'll let 'em go; Two Toes will take care of them. I don't know where that old Indian's at, but you can bet he's watching from somewhere. No, we'll not worry 'bout the first ones; we'll wait for the second bunch to try to cross, and when they do, we'll let 'em get right in the middle; then we'll open up. What happens after that is anybody's guess; we'll just have to wait and see."

The men at the bottom started their horses, and as Elam had mentioned, Roscoe led the group of men slowly toward the next line of trees. There they drew up and stepped from their saddles and were not long in building a campfire, and a short time later they all sat around it drinking coffee. Elam had the idea that not only were they drinking coffee around that fire, but Roscoe was also taking this time to lay out his plan, and it would not be long before all hell broke lose. Elam also got the notion, by the way Roscoe kept looking— letting his eyes slowly scan the mountainside—that he watched for a wisp of dust, a puff of smoke or even a flicker off a gun-barrel, anything that would let him know that he had found the right place. But on the other hand, Elam was sure that Roscoe had already noticed the buzzards flying and had probably already spotted some of the pieces of clothing that hung on many of the branches where they had been caught after being picked up by the wind.

Another hour went by before there was any more movement; all of a sudden they all stood, and after walking to their horses they mounted. Elam could see Roscoe standing tall in the saddle pointing to several of the men, and as Elam had expected four men broke from the group and rode toward the clearing.

"He's sending four," Elam said. "I figured two but four will be okay. Might be a bit much for Two Toes to handle all by himself though. One of us might need to go give 'im a hand."

"I'll go," Luke answered.

"Just hold on there, Luke," Elam called out. "Let's wait and see for sure what they're going to do. Anyway if someone goes, he needs to have two good legs. I thank you for your offer, but if someone goes it needs to be me or Cork."

The four men rode slowly up the hill for the first hundred yards or so, working their way between the rocks and around the big patches of prickly-pear and the thorny, twisted branches of the many mesquite. As they reached the edge of the clearing, they ran the gut-hooks to their horses and crossed it at a full-out run. Roscoe sat on his horse beside Frank Clancy and watched the four men make their way across the clearing but seemed a bit aggravated when there was no gunfire. He reached up and disappointingly stripped the hat from his head and mopped at the sweat with a sleeve.

"I see Roscoe and Frank," Cork said in a low voice. "But I sure don't see Bill Powers. I wonder where he's at?"

"I don't know," Elam answered. "I was kinda wondering the same thing. It's not like 'im not to be here."

Then Roscoe did something that Elam had not planned on—he touched his horse forward.

"Well I'll be darned," Elam mumbled. "Him and Frank are coming with 'em—I'd never figured on that." Bringing his rifle up, he said, "Okay, men, get ready. This may be our one chance to end this thing once and for all right now."

Like the men who had gone before them they rode slow taking their time still not quite sure, then right at the edge of the clearing Roscoe drew up and sat for a long moment. Turning to Frank, he said something that must've been funny because both men let out a big roaring belly laugh. Then Roscoe touched his horse with an easy spur and with Clancy still beside him, they rode into the middle of the group of men. There, again he drew up. Reaching he pulled his hat down tight on his head, and with that done, he kicked his horse and took a double slap with the reins.

"Wait until they're in the middle," Elam called out.

Luke held his fire for what seemed to be hours, but in reality it couldn't have been over a few seconds. Just as the charging men reached the center of the clearing they all three pulled the triggers. Instantly the three men riding out front threw up their hand and tumbled from their horses. Elam, then drew his sights on the chest of Frank Clancy, knowing that with Frank out of the way he could maybe get a shot at Roscoe. He steadied the gun and pulled the trigger. The bullet flew and as it entered Frank's body there was a loud pop, and the impact drove Frank backward forcing him to grab at the pommel with both hands, but it was too late. He was dead, and with life gone, he fell from his horse. With the roar of the other two guns two more men fell from their horses, and the four that trailed along behind swung around and headed back for the trees. Elam worked the lever feeding another bullet into the chamber and quickly zeroed in on Roscoe, but just as he pulled the trigger his horse jumped over a rock and the bullet struck Roscoe high on the left leg. Moments later, he disappeared behind the cliff wall.

Turning from the line of cedar, Elam broke into a dead run and at the same time called out, "Loraine, give me a loaded gun." As he ran by, she pitched it to him. He made his way along the trail running as fast as he could. At the gravel bed, he slowed to a walk and when he got to the creek, he stopped. After giving everything a good close look, he made his way over the stepping stones. Stopping again, he turned an ear to the wind and could hear Cork coming along the trail behind him. From across the meadow to the north and a little east several shots rang out. Apparently Two Toes had the first four men penned down, and from the sound of things he was giving 'em hell. But where was Roscoe—and how bad was he hit? Had he made it all the way down to where the shooting was taking place or had he somehow figured it to be a trap and stopped short hoping to cut across and find the camp. If he had, how many men would he have with him. Elam knew that the ridge was not passable on horseback anywhere along in here. Not until you got to the break in the wall on the far side could you ride through, but a man could, if he was on foot and in good enough shape to do a little climbing, cross it anywhere. He gazed in the direction of the horses grazing in the meadow, and they all stood with their heads up high, their ears perked looking in the direction of the gunfire. I need to get over there and help Two Toes out, he thought to himself. But hearing Cork coming over the stepping stones, he walked back toward the creek. "I'm going on over and see if I can help Two Toes out. Cork, why don't you go back and set up somewhere just this side of the bottleneck and watch the trail. Did Luke stay in camp with Loraine?"

"He was still there when I took out after you." Cork answered, pointing back toward camp. "He was going to stay and keep an eye on those four or five men that turned back—to make sure they didn't try to cross the clearing again."

"That's good," Elam replied. "Now you head on back and watch that bottleneck." Turning, Elam cast his eyes upon the open meadow; from one side to the other there was absolutely nothing a man could use for cover—not a rock or tree anywhere. So thinking it best not to attempt it, he started off at a right angle along the tree line. He knew he had to move quick, but not so quick that he might walk into something he couldn't get out of—like the sights of Roscoe's gun. Coming to the first place he could turn back north, he did, and with each step he took now, he was getting closer to the gunfire. At the same time the sun was dropping behind the mountain throwing a dark-gray haze over the little meadow and everything around it. Elam walked on knowing that time was running out, for soon it would be dark—and that would mean having to get in close to kill someone needing to be killed. Only fifty yards or so from where the majority of the gunfire was coming from, he turned east, and after working his way through a thick entanglement of briars, he made his way to the edge of the ridge and looked over. There within sixty yards, holed up in an outcropping of rocks, was two of the first four men. Elam, quickly let his eyes scan the surrounding rocks, and trees in search of the other two but unable to see anything of them, he turned his attention back to the two that were penned down. They seemed to be taking turns shooting at Two Toes, and while one shot back, the other was desperately looking around for a way out. But now that Elam was in place there was no way out. They only had but one choice and that was to die. He raised his gun and brought the sights in line with one of the men's back and pulled the trigger. The impact drove the man's body hard against the rock which he hid behind. The other one, seeing his buddy fall and hearing the shot, turned, and when he did Two Toes shot him in the back of the head. Elam lay motionless for a long while, his eyes searching along the trail for the other two, but unable to locate anyone else, he stood and walking slow, and hunkered down through the trees, he started back toward camp. But he knew that somewhere between where he now walked and his destination, Roscoe and at least two maybe three more men had to be waiting and it was getting dark. But there was no need in hurrying for he knew that Luke had stayed in camp with Loraine and Cork, at this very moment, was watching the trail. *But if I can just make it back to the bottleneck,* he thought to himself, *then Roscoe will have to come to me.* He moved on slow and easy—his eyes focused trying to see in the dim light—his ears turned to the wind straining to hear, but within minutes total darkness had fallen upon the meadow and what little sight he'd had to this point was no more. Knowing that he was now within just two hundred yards of the creek crossing, he pushed on. All of a sudden for some strange reason his mind told him to *stop*, and he did and stood perfectly still in the darkness. He listened and what he heard was scary for what he heard was nothing—not one frog—not one insect—not one bird— not one anything. Slowly, he took a step and his mind screamed out, *Stop and stay put until morning!* Suddenly realizing that it was not his mind doing the talking, but rather his instinct, Elam, without moving another inch, dropped to the ground beside a tree. He sat motionless trying to remember what he'd heard or thought he had heard to stop him, or was it that he was just getting old and knew that his hearing or his sight for that matter were not what they used to be. Hell, that old Indian sneaking up on me like he did the other morning proved that, he thought to himself. Taking a deep, ragged breath, he let it out slow. Suddenly he heard something—over to his left—a low murmur or maybe a groan or maybe it was someone trying to whisper to somebody. Elam held his breath to listen more closely, but for a good long bit he heard nothing else; then there it was again—a low whisper, it was someone talking to someone else, of that he was now sure—but who? His pulse quickened as he reached down for his pistol butt, but then, thinking of the noise a shot would make, he reached around to his left side and felt for the handle of his knife. Sliding it from the scabbard, he placed it carefully between his teeth, then rolled over onto all fours, and with all the quietness and skills a mountain lion would use in stalking an injured deer, Elam slowly started to crawl, moving one hand at a time then one leg at a time, as he moved ever so slowly through the tangled underbrush in the direction of the voices. A time or two razor-sharp thorns dug into his skin or got caught in his clothing bringing him to a stop, but after working himself loose, he crawled on. At times, the voices would raise slightly above a whisper giving Elam a little better sense of direction. Coming to two giant old trees that grew side by side within a few inches of each other, he stopped to listen. There were three voices all together. One of the voices seemed to moan continually—obviously from pain brought on by some sort of wound.

"If you don't shut 'im up," the first voice said, "I'm goin' to kill 'im."

"He's dying," the second voice replied. "It won't be long."

"Well, hell," the first voice sneered. "Can't you do somethin' to keep 'im quiet until he does. If nothing else, put your hand over his mouth. If you don't shut 'im up, somebody's going to hear 'im."

"I'm doing all I can do," the second voice answered. "That gut-shot has got to be hurtin' like the devil—ripped 'im wide open. If it wasn't for 'im holdin' 'em in, his guts would fall out."

"I wonder where Roscoe's is?" the first voice questioned. "He said he'd be back."

"Hell, you know where he's at," the second voice answered. "He's gone after that damn old tracker—that Elam Langtry feller. Why do you reckon Roscoe's wantin' to kill 'im so bad? That's all he talks about."

"I know why," the first voice replied. "That old buzzard made 'im look like a fool, that's why. Roscoe followed that false trail all the way to Caster. Men like him don't get over being made a fool of none too soon. I'd hate to be in that old man's boots when Roscoe does find 'im."

"Oh, I don't know too much 'bout that," the second voice cut in. "Looks to me like that old man as you call 'im and that bunch with 'im are doing a pretty fair job of holding their own. We're all that's left out of thirteen men."

"Yeah," the first voice replied. "But if those other four or five cowards that turned back would have come on we'd had 'em."

"I don't think it would have changed anything," the second voice said. "All it would have changed is the number of dead bodies. There would have been just that many more dead men."

"No more talking," the first voice ordered. "You're startin' to get on my nerves, and if I don't kill you first, Roscoe will if he hear's you talkin' any such way."

"It don't really matter who stops me from breathin'," the second voice replied, then after a lengthy pause, he added, " 'Cause I think we all died the minute we stepped foot on this mountain."

Once again it was quiet, but during the two men's short conversation the third man had died because his moans could be heard no more. But during that time Elam had learned the men doing the talking were just on the other side of those two big trees. The big question was, where was Roscoe. Had he left these men here and moved on toward the creek in hopes of making his way to the flat, or had he left them here knowing they would talk thinking that Elam or someone else might hear them and in doing so draw them into a trap. Had Roscoe really gone or was he sitting somewhere close by in the darkness, waiting for Elam to make his move on the three men, hoping he might speak or in approaching step on a twig and snap it, hoping for anything with sound so he might get a lucky shot in the dark.

After giving all the possibilities much careful thought, Elam decided to go ahead and kill these two, and after making up his mind to do so, he quietly turned to his left and started inching his way ever so slowly around the tree. He moved one hand at a time, making sure he removed all the dried leaves and twigs from under it before he put it down, then the other and at the same time making sure his knees dropped to the same spot his hand had just been picked up. With the knife gripped between his teeth, he crawled on but suddenly his pulse raced as his hand touched what felt to be a boot—the dead man's boot. He slowly let his hand move along the piece of leather, then along the pant-leg to his waist, there the body started angling up like maybe the man's head was propped up on something. Elam slowly run his hand along the ground until he felt another leg running crossways of the body and he knew then, that one of the other men was sitting there, holding the dead man's head in his lap. Elam, slowly moved into position to where he'd be within easy reach of his victim. Then estimating about where he thought the man's head to be, he moved both hands at one time, cupping his left hand over the man's mouth and with the right, he drew the blade across his throat. The man's arms came up but it was too late and the only sound made was a slight guzzle as the blood and air gushed from the opening.

"Roscoe, is that you?" the other man whispered.

Elam turned at the sound of the voice and plunged the knife hard through the darkness and as it ripped its way through the man's chest, his body jerked. Elam reached and pulled the man's head close and whispered in his ear. "No, it ain't Roscoe. It's Elam Langtry, the old tracker." He gave the knife a good, hard, final twist. When the man had re-laxed, Elam let him lay over on the ground; then wiping the blood from the blade on the man's shirt, he placed it back in the scabbard. He sat for a long while listening but heard no sound. If Roscoe is somewhere close, he thought to himself, he's not moving—not as much as breathing. But knowing he would not be safe here if Roscoe did return, Elam decided to change locations, so after crawling back around the tree and finding his Winchester, he once again began to crawl, but coming to the second tree over, he stopped there and leaned his back against the trunk. He thought briefly of much needed sleep but knew with Roscoe running loose that if he closed his eyes even for just a short while, he might not ever open them again. He had to stay awake—he had to keep his ears keen to the sounds around him.

The night seemed to linger, but its complete darkness was ended by just a few rays of light, and as the sun rose in the east the blackness changed into gray then the gray into light. Elam, after giving his surroundings a quick check, reached up and grabbed a low limb and pulled him-self slowly up straight. Crossing to where the bodies of the three men lay, he toed them over one at a time to find he had never seen the men before. But then, he noticed some-thing that made his blood run cold—the body of a fourth man sat with his back leaning against a tree, no more than five feet east of the two big trees that Elam had crawled around. It was Roscoe Nash; he sat holding his gun in his hand. Apparently he had left the others and moved over to wait; blood stained the grass and ground where it had run from the wound on his leg, and he had sat there and bled out. Seeing a paper sticking out from his coat pocket, Elam reached and took it, and after shaking it loose, he read it.

It was from Laughlin and gave Roscoe Nash half of all he owned. A cold chill washed over Elam as he realized how close he had come; he had to have been within inches of the man when he crawled by. Tipping his hat, he said, "You'll never know how close you came." Turning, he stuck the paper deep into his own pocket and started toward camp. At the creek, he made his way over the stepping stones, and along the trail to the gravel bed where his brother emerged from the brush. "We'll rest up today and start for home in the morning."

"How 'bout Roscoe?" Cork asked.

"We won't be worrying about Roscoe Nash anymore," Elam replied. "He's dead. The only one we have to worry about now is Laughlin, and if Roscoe or somebody else ain't killed Bill Powers for some reason, he's still in the game."

Shoulder to shoulder the two men walked on to camp where Luke and Loraine waited. "How 'bout the men in the bottom," Elam asked talking to Luke. "Are they still down there?"

"They stayed until this morning," Luke answered. "But they high-tailed it out of here at first light. They're probably back in Rising Star by now."

"They won't go back to Rising Star, or at least I know I wouldn't go back," Cork said. "That's the last place I'd want to be after cuttin' out on Roscoe like they did, and they don't know he's dead yet."

"Here, y'all look at this paper," Elam said taking it from his pocket. "It says here that Laughlin gave Roscoe half of all he owns. But with Roscoe dead it all goes right back to Laughlin now."

"He won't have it long either," Luke cut in. " 'Cause I'm

killin' Maxwell Laughlin first thing when I get back to town."

Elam gave an understanding nod, and said, "That's sure okay by me, but you might have Bill Powers to kill too, and no telling how many more will be with 'im. For sure he wasn't with this bunch. Hopefully he's already dead, but I wouldn't count on it."

"Well, anyhow," Cork broke in, "we might as well get everything picked up around here so we'll be ready to start down the hill in the morning. Me and Loraine need to get back, we've got a ranch to look after."

Elam smiled at his brother's words. On his way under the overhang he thought, *I wonder what Laughlin and Bill Powers have got in store for us.*

Chapter Eight

Laughlin slid his chair back and pushed up slowly from the table. Looking across at Bill Powers, he asked, "You 'bout ready?"

"Why?" Bill questioned in his usual dry tone. "You in a hurry to get in bed?"

"No, no," Laughlin replied. "I just need to stop by the office real quick and take care of some paper work." Looking over, he asked, "How was your steak, Bill? Was it cooked to your liking?"

"Just right," Bill answered rubbing at his belly with both hands. "Yes, sir, that steak was mighty fine." Glancing up, he smiled and said, "You know, Laughlin, I could sure get used to living like this."

Laughlin smiled back, but the smile was only to conceal his ever-growing hatred for this man, and he knew that if he could only somehow stay alive for a couple more days things would change. Perkins and Bear should be getting

163

here, and then, he would show Bill Powers what he really thought about him living at all, much less like this. Laughlin took some money from his wallet and pitched it down on the table. Leading the way to the door, he walked from the café out onto the boardwalk. Laughlin looked up the street. "Say, Bill," he said throwing up a hand. "Why don't you mosey on down to the Ann Mayre and see what's going on down there. I'll go on over to the Driftwood and take care of my paper work. There's really no need in you staying with me all the time. I'm not going to do anything that you wouldn't approve of."

"I know you ain't, Laughlin, but I kinda wish you would. That way I could go ahead and kill you and wouldn't have to dog after you all the time. Thanks for the offer, but Roscoe told me to watch you. And you know I kinda try to do what Roscoe tells me to do. If he knew that I had old Smitty watching you at night while I got a little sleep, he'd be after my hide for sure. You know that, but you'd never tell 'im, would you?"

Laughlin shook his head. "Bill, you know I ain't going to say nothing."

Bill gave a loud roaring laugh and slapped his hands together. Stepping from the boardwalk the two men crossed the wide dirt street in the direction of the Driftwood. After pushing through the batwing doors, Laughlin let his eyes quickly search the room in hopes of seeing two new faces—but to his dismay there was none. Maybe tomorrow, he thought to himself. Turning to Bill, he asked, "You want something to drink? If you do I'll get us a bottle."

"I don't know why you'd even asked me that, Maxwell. You know damn good and well that I want something to drink." Stepping up to the bar, Bill called out. "Hank, give me a bottle of your best whisky and my good friend Maxwell Laughlin here is buying."

"Bill, go ahead and help yourself," Laughlin said, walking in the direction of his office. Getting to the door, he turned back and said, "Get us a table over there somewhere, and I'll be back before you know it."

Bill spun and drew his gun and as he did, he called out. "Laughlin, you touch that doorknob and I'm going to kill you before you can turn it."

"I told you, Bill, there's some paper work in there I need to take care of."

"I don't give a damn what you told me. What I'm telling you is, if you touch that door I'm going to shoot you—and I'm going to shoot you dead. Do you understand me?"

All talking suddenly stopped, and the old piano went silent. All that could be heard was the sliding back of chairs and the sound of footsteps as everyone jumped up and moved against the wall, getting out of the line of fire. A dead quiet fell over the smoke-filled room as they waited to see what Laughlin was going to do. No one had ever seen Maxwell Laughlin called out, but they had all seen him call several—no one special though—only men he knew he could handle, like a few of the town drunks, and of course, he'd had a couple of run-ins with Leroy Radford, the used-to-be sheriff. But now against a top gun-hand—a man who if not for Laughlin himself bringing him here wouldn't even be in town—he seemed to have lost most of his fight and all his nerve.

Laughlin forced a faint smile. "C'mon, Bill," he said. "There's no need in all of that. If you don't want me to go in the office, then I'll stay out here and have a drink with you. Those papers can wait till morning."

"You're right they can. If I say they'll wait—they'll

wait," Powers replied. "Now if you know what's good for you, Laughlin, you'll get over here, sit down, and have a drink." Bill holstered his Colt; then taking the bottle and two glasses from the bar, he walked over and dropped down to a chair.

Laughlin jerked a handkerchief from his inside coat pocket and nervously mopped the cold sweat from his stiff, pale face. Motioning with a shaky hand toward the old piano, he said, "Let's have some music." Then he yelled out, "Belly up to the bar, boys! The drinks are on me." He had only taken a couple of steps toward the table where Bill had ordered him to sit, when the batwing doors swung open, and Laughlin looked up—as did every person in the place—to see two strangers walking in.

The first to enter was a tall, thin man, well over six feet, with long, collar-length, red hair. He wore a black coat and pants, and a white shirt that were covered thick with trail dust, and a black flat crown hat with a hatband made from the skin of a rattlesnake. But what caught Laughlin's eye most was the six-gun he wore swung low and tied to his leg.

The second man was shorter by a good six inches, but wider across the shoulders, with a full shock of neatly trimmed black hair and mustache. He was dressed much in the same fashion, with a black coat and pants and white shirt, and like the first man he was covered from head to toe with dust. But what really set him apart from the first man were the two pearl-handled .44s he wore with the butts turned foward.

The two men walked deeper into the room and drew up at the bar. "Barkeep, two shots of your best," the taller of the two called out. But apparently changing his mind, he said, "On second thought, just bring us a bottle and two glasses."

Hank was not long in getting them what they had ordered. Walking from the bar the two men found a table near the back and sat down. After tossing down the first two drinks one right after the other, they poured a third, and with the trail dust washed from their dry throats, they seemed content to sip.

Laughlin looked at the two men in wonder. It was apparent that both were gunfighters, or at least they dressed the part, wanting people to think they were. But to him they looked awful young—neither appearing to be a day over twenty-five years. Was this Sam Perkins and Max Bear, the two men he had sent for? Surely not, he thought to himself; men of their reputation would have to be much older. On the other hand he could not just dismiss the idea on their appearance alone, for he had never met them himself and knew only of the two men that he'd been told by his good friend Porky Farley. A man who, Laughlin knew for a fact, had just three years ago brought in Bear and Perkins to head up a land takeover much like he himself was trying to do in Rising Star. They had gotten it done and done well—doing away with all that the ranchers and townsfolk could throw at them. And it had all happened in a little town just a few miles south of San Antonio, one that is now called Farley, Texas. If these were the two men he waited for—on whom his life depended—how was he going to get word to them—how was he to let them know that their first job would be to kill the man who sat across the table from him—the one who sat smiling and who was drinking whisky from the same bottle.

Flo wasted no time moving in and taking a seat on the taller one's knee, and before the two newcomers had finished their third drink, she had moved into her own chair between them and had poured herself a drink from their bottle and they were all laughing and carrying on like three old friends. When the laughter had finally faded, the taller one reached up and pulled her head close and whispered something in her ear. When she straighten back in her seat she faintly pointed toward Maxwell Laughlin's table, then turning back to the man said something under her breath. That's when Laughlin knew that these were the two men he'd been waiting for.

Powers, noticing Laughlin's long stare, asked, "What's wrong, Maxwell, you a mite jealous over that fancy girl sittin' with those other two fellers?"

Laughlin looked over but didn't answer. Instead he raised his glass high and said, "Here's to you, Powers. May you have a short and miserable life." Smiling, he brought the glass up to his lips and took a sip.

"Now, Laughlin, it hurts to hear you say things like that," Bill responded dryly. "And to show you there's no hard feelings, I'm going to wish you a long and happy life, but you know as will as I do that it just ain't going to happen."

"Oh, I don't know 'bout that, Bill. I might fool you. I might live longer than you think. I might just live to be an old man."

The sudden sound of chairs being slid back drew their attention, and they looked toward the back to see the two strangers getting to their feet.

"I think I'll have a beer," Laughlin said pushing up from the table, then looking down at Bill, he asked, "You want one?"

"No," he answered, looking in the direction of the two men. He had noticed something in the change of their expressions that had stirred his suspicion, and now he sat paying very little attention to what Laughlin was doing and more to the two men walking toward him.

Not wanting to be anywhere near the table or Bill Powers if and when the gunplay started, Laughlin moved slowly but with much urgency toward the bar. Then, he turned and looked back just as the two men drew up stopping just short of the table. The tall one glanced over in Laughlin's direction. And Laughlin looked at Bill and nodded his head.

"You've got my seat," the tall one said to Bill in a voice that was cold and hard. Standing with his feet spread wide, he threw his coat-tail back and positioned his hand over the butt of his gun and said, "You need to get up and move on or fill your hand."

"I don't move for nobody," Bill replied through gritted teeth. "Is it just going to be me and you, or do I have to fight both of you?" he asked getting to his feet.

"It makes no difference," the tall one scoffed, his eyes locked on Bill's. "You're dead either way."

Bill's eyes narrowed, and for the longest time they did not blink. Reaching up, he rubbed at his mustache and after giving it a careful twist on the ends said, "Son, you don't know who you're messing with. Maybe you've heard of me. My name is Bill Powers; I ride with Roscoe Nash."

"Well, since we're introducing ourselves," the tall one said. "My name is Max Bear and this little short fellow here is Sam Perkins, and as of right now, Mr. Powers, we both work for Mr. Maxwell Laughlin over there and I'm athinking he wants you dead."

Bill dropped his hand for his gun, but the tall man's hand was the quicker, and he sent a bullet ripping right between Bill's eyes. At the same instant the short man fanned two more shots into Bill's body, both finding their marks dead center of each pocket on his shirt. On stiff legs, Bill staggered back a couple of steps; his face went white, and he stood for a moment surprised, for he knew that his gun had not even cleared leather. Finally his knees buckled and he fell face down on the floor—and lay dead.

"Good shootin'," Laughlin called out from the bar, then slowly drawing his own gun, he flung open the cylinder and raised it high above his head to show everyone it was empty. "When Powers called me," Laughlin announced, "I couldn't do anything 'cause I didn't have any shells in my gun, and that buzzard knew it." Motioning toward the dead man, he said, "Some of you men drag him out of here before he stains the floor." Looking back, he called out in a happy voice, "Hank, me and Mr. Bear and Mr. Perkins are going to my office; bring us a new bottle and some glasses."

Hank gave a nod and answered, "Okay, Mr. Laughlin."

Grabbing each of the two men by the hand, Laughlin gave them a shake. Then turning, he led them through the door into his office. "You boys did one heck of a fine job out there," Laughlin said, taking a seat behind his desk.

"We aim to please," Sam Perkins answered with a smile. "Now how 'bout the ten thousand dollars?"

"Got it right across the street in the bank. We can go get it now or first thing in the morning when I open up. It's up to you." Giving a laugh, he added, "Yeah, old Bill didn't even know what hit 'im—and I just fed 'im a dollar steak, too."

"We can wait until morning on the money," Max said, looking over at Sam. "But for now why don't you kinda explain to us what we're up against."

"Well, boys, there's really not no whole lot to say," Laughlin began. "I started out just needing to have a man named Luke Ludd killed, and maybe Cork and Elam Langtry and Cork's girl Loraine, so I could take over their land, but now that Roscoe's turned on me like he has, things have changed a mite. There's him and Frank Clancy, Heath Benson. You've done killed Bill Powers, and I may need you to kill Leroy Radford, for me too. Leroy used to be the sheriff here and he knows some things I don't need him telling, but if you don't want to kill him then that's okay. I can take care of him myself—oh, yeah, there's Barton and Quint McKuen too, and there may be one or two more, but I'll let you known more about them as the days go by. Barton and Quint are out with Roscoe and the others right now looking for Ludd and that bunch—hell, half of 'em may already be dead as far as I know."

"That's a hell of a lot of killing," Sam said, looking up from under the brim of his hat. "What's the law going to be doing while all the shootin' is going on?"

"I just told you. Leroy Radford used to be our sheriff, but he's out. And his deputy has completely left the country. I don't even know where he's gone. So there's no law here. The nearest law is all the way over in Caster a good two days ride from here. Hey look, boys, I'm not only paying you ten thousand dollars each, but I'm going to furnish you a nice place to stay and all you can eat and drink, and if you want female company you can have your pick from any of those girls right outside the door there or down the street at the Ann Mayre. I own 'em all. Go ahead and help yourselves. All you got to do is be here and be ready if and when I need you."

"Sounds like a good plan to me," Sam said. Looking over, he asked, "How 'bout you, Max? What do you make of it?"

A big smile came to Max Bear's face. Reaching, he rubbed at the week's growth of heavy stubble along his jaw; then standing, he smiled and asked, "Where's those rooms?"

Luke walked from under the overhang in the direction of the bottleneck where he would relieve Cork of his guard duty. He walked slow in the cool night air, his belly full of good hot rabbit stew. His mind somewhat relieved now that the worst of the fighting was over. Maybe everyone could get some rest. He thought of the upcoming morning and the long ride back to Rising Star and the job that still lay ahead. *Yes, if it is my power I will kill Maxwell Laughlin,* he thought to himself, *for the death of my father, and then and only then will my job be finished—but how many will have to die before I get to him?* Noticing there was no more limp when he walked, he turned his eyes toward the heavens and thanked God that he was going back to Rising Star in better shape than he had left it in. Getting to the gravel bed, he slowed. At the big rock where Elam had left him the first night, he stopped, and cupping his hands around his mouth, he called out in a low voice, "Flour sack."

"Empty," Cork's voice called back. Moments later in the darkness Luke felt Cork's hand come in contact with his shoulder. "I don't think we're going to have any more trouble tonight," Cork whispered. "But after making it this far I'd hate to let our guard down too soon. We know those four that turned back are gone, but we don't know to where or how far. And where is that Bill Powers?"

"Cork, I sure do want to thank you for helping me out the way you did, and I'm sorry I caused you all this trouble."

"Luke, you didn't cause us any trouble. Laughlin was coming after us anyway, but having you along I think it helped us make the right choices. Like coming up here. Without you being shot up the way you were, we'd never come this far. Now I just hope we can finish this deal off. I imagine you're wanting to get back to your job."

"Yes, sir, I sure am, and I'll be dragging out as soon as I get Laughlin taken care of."

"What are you going to do with your paw's place?" Cork asked. "Sell it?"

"No, I don't think so. I was thinking 'bout maybe giving it to Loraine."

A long silence fell between the two men, then it was Luke who asked, "You think she'd want it?"

"I don't know," Cork answered. "That's something you'll have to talk to her about." Turning, he walked off along the dark trail leading to camp.

The night went without a hitch, and shortly after sunup, they had the pack horses loaded and ready to go. Taking with them only what Loraine figured it would take to get them home, they left the rest for the old Indian.

Two Toes had the day before rounded up all the horses he could find belonging to the dead men. He was going to keep half for himself and send the rest back with Cork along with a whole load of guns and saddles.

Cork shook Two Toes' hand. Then just before stepping into leather, he looked back and said, "Thanks Two Toes, I'll see you when the weather turns."

"Hunting may be good in the fall and if not I have many horses to sell," the old Indian answered. "Maybe not need to come." Turning to Elam, he said, "Next time you here, me show you how to walk like cat, make no noise."

"Why, you old sidewinder," Elam replied, giving him a playful slap on the back. "I may just take you up on that, or maybe I'll just show up one of these days to talk. How would that be?"

The old Indian smiled for the first time. "You come and sit at my fire anytime." Turning to Luke, he said, "Take care of your woman; she'll give you many sons."

Luke's face flashed red with embarrassment, and without looking at Loraine or the old Indian and without speaking another word, he swung up to leather. Throwing up a good-bye hand, they started across the little meadow. Their descent from the mountain was easier and faster than coming up since they weren't dragging a sick man on a travois. They made such good time that they made camp that night where they had left the wagon, and the next morning they hitched up the team and started for home.

Elam and Luke rode out front, their eyes constantly searching the hills to east and west and the trail ahead for signs. Their nerves never relaxed and their guns were always at the ready. Loraine drove the wagon with some of the extra horses tied to it, and Cork rode behind leading the rest. On the second day, a fast-moving thunderstorm with high wind and small hail forced them to seek shelter in a stand of oak. After the storm had gone past, they decided to make camp. But the next morning well before first light, they packed up and hit the trail again, knowing that if everything went well they should be home by dark. Just as the last few rays from the setting sun faded behind the western horizon they topped the hill, and at the bottom was home. But Elam, noticing a column of white smoke coming up from the chimney, drew up and stopped the wagon. "Looks like we've got company," he said to Luke. Turning in the saddle, he called out, "Cork, you stay here with Loraine and the wagon. Me and Luke will go on in and have a look. If you hear gunfire turn around and head back north, we'll catch up with you later." Together the two men rode off down the hill. At about the half way point Elam drew up, and after studying the situation for a short moment said, "Luke, you swing around and come in on the back side of the house. I'll cut through the trees and come up behind the barn." After a long silent pause, he added, "Watch yourself, Luke; it might be Bill Powers, and if it is, there's no telling how many men he'll have with 'im."

"You do the same," Luke answered. Then touching his horse with a spur, he broke from the trail and rode east. Elam turned west, and riding a trail he knew well and had ridden several times over the last five years, he worked around to the back of the barn. Sliding slowly to the ground, he tied up at the corral fence. With the dim light of dusk quickly fading, he made his way along the side of the barn to where he could see through the lighted window of the house. After watching for a long while and not seeing any movement on the inside, he made his way, slow and hunkered down, across the yard to the corner of the house. There Elam eased his way along the wall until he came to the window. Removing his hat, he peeked through a small gap between the curtains to see Luke standing in the middle of the parlor floor with his gun drawn and at his feet lay a man who looked a whole lot like the sheriff, Leroy Radford. Taking a quick look around and not seeing anyone else, Elam made his way up the steps and through the door. "Who have we got here?" he asked.

"That lying sheriff of Rising Star. That good-for-nothing Leroy Radford," Luke answered. "The one that told everybody that I shot Clint, Porter, and Robert McKuen down in cold blood."

"Hold on, Luke!" Leroy cried out. "Give me a chance to explain. I had to say it. Laughlin would have killed me if

I hadn't. I know they tried to ambush you—hell, I was there—remember? But I've already been over to Caster and sent a wire to have the warrants dropped. I don't know what else to do, but to say I'm sorry. I've been out here three days waiting—hoping you'd show up. They're waiting for you in town, Luke; if you show up there they're going to kill all of you."

"Who," Luke asked. "Bill Powers?

"Lord no, Bill's dead. No, it's two new fellers that Laughlin hired. They rode into town three days ago; the one calling himself Max Bear shot Bill right between the eyes and that other fellow with 'im—I think his name is Sam Perkins—shot 'im two more times dead center of his shirt pockets before Bill could clear leather. Since then they've just kinda been hanging around town waiting for you or Roscoe and his bunch to show. I think Laughlin hired 'em to kill Barton and Quint too. And I'm sure he's wanting me dead."

"They might get a shot at you, Leroy," Elam said. "But they won't be shootin' at none of those other fellows you named 'cause they're all dead. We left 'em all lying back there on Beaver Mountain." Turning to Luke, Elam said, "You go on back and get Cork and the wagon, I'll stay here and keep the sheriff company."

When Luke returned with the wagon, they put their horses in the barn and gave them hay and grain. Then they turned the extra horses loose on the green grass that grew tall in the little trap just north of the barn.

Luke helped Elam hang the harness over the pegs in the tack room. "I think maybe I'll head on into town after we have a bite of supper," he said.

"I've been giving this deal some thought, Luke," Elam answered. "We may not want to go tonight, but maybe wait and go first thing in the morning while they're hopefully still in bed. If those boys are that fast with their guns, then we don't need no showdown. We need to use our heads. I know you're wantin' to get this deal over with, but if'n I was you I'd kinda slow down and think it over. Luke, I've heard that you're awful fast with that there gun of yours, and I don't doubt it for a minute, but there's two of them that we know about and no telling how many more, and me and old Cork in there—well, if you ain't noticed, let me tell you, we ain't gunslingers."

"What have you got in mind, Elam?"

"Well, I'm figuring that the main ones, like Laughlin and those two gunfighters, Perkins and Bear, will all be holdup in the same place—upstairs in those big, nice, fancy rooms at the Driftwood, but as you know there's eight of those rooms up there, and we only know that Laughlin is in the first one there at the top of the stairs."

"Won't they have somebody watching the street?" Luke cut in. "And you know as well as I do that the door to the Driftwood will be locked."

"Now you're using your head, Luke," Elam said with a smile. "But here's the other part of our puzzle. Old Hank, the barkeep, stays in the storeroom and has ever since he went to work there. That's who we need to talk to because he knows which rooms the other two men are staying in. If we can get 'im to open that back door, there where they unload the whisky barrels from the wagons, then we can enter the saloon through the door between his room and the bar."

"Elam, it sounds good, but there's sure a lot of ifs and ands there."

"Well, if it don't work, Luke, we can always do it the other way and just go to shootin'."

"Okay," Luke replied. "All we can do is give it a try and see."

Before daylight the four men led their horses from the barn, and just before stepping in to leather, Cork turned to his daughter and said, "Loraine, I want you to get up there in the loft and don't come down until we get back, and if we're not back by nightfall I want you to get on your horse and go to Caster and catch the next stage to anywhere, but don't stay here."

"Oh, Paw," Loraine said throwing her arms around his neck. "Ain't there some other way? Please don't go into town. Those men are gunfighters; they'll kill you, Paw. Let's all go to Caster and catch the stage; we can all go somewhere and start over."

"I could never live with myself if we did it that way, Loraine, and you know that. No, I've got to go, but don't worry I'll be back. You just go on and do like I told you and get in the loft." Taking her in his arms, he gave her a little kiss on the forehead and said, "I love you, girl."

"I love you too, Paw." Turning she looked up and said, "Be careful, Luke." Then throwing her arms around his neck, she did something that took them all by surprise. She brought his head down and gave him a kiss on the lips and as their lips parted, she whispered, "I love you, Luke; please be careful."

Elam seeing the way Loraine was taking on, didn't want no part of it, so he kicked his horse forward and started along the dark trail, then throwing up an unseen hand, he called out, "I'll have 'em back by supper."

The four men rode at a canter through the darkness, not slowing their pace until they reached the bridge on the west end of town. There they slid to the ground and tied their horses to the old cottonwood. Elam turned to Leroy and instructed him to stay with the horse and not to make a sound. With Elam leading, they made their way south for a hundred yards or so; then swinging back east they approached the back of the livery stable from the south, but as they did a horse in the corral nickered sending all three men to their bellies on the ground. After a bit, Elam pushed up to his feet; then motioning with a hand for the others to follow, he continued on to the back of the livery stable. Walking parallel to the street, he made his way past the back doors of the Ann Mayre, the hotel, newspaper, and the saddle shop. Coming to the Driftwood, he stopped.

Knowing that a loud knock might wake Laughlin or the other men, he tapped lightly on the door with only a knuckle, but after not getting a response, he tapped a little harder. This time he heard movement but no one came. He knocked a little harder, and again he heard someone stir inside, and then he saw a candle flicker. Moments later the door latch moved with a thud, and the door opened to only a crack. "Who is it?" a voice asked groggily—a woman's voice.

"Flo, is that you?" Elam asked. "Flo, it's Elam Langtry. I need to talk to you, open up and let me in."

"No more tonight, I'm too tired, come back tomorrow."

"No, Flo, it's nothing like that. I just need to talk to you—where's Hank? Is he in there with you?" She must have relaxed her grip on the door or turned away to look back or maybe say something to Hank, but when Elam felt the pressure on the door lessen, he pushed it open and walked in.

At the sudden force, Flo, took a couple of unsettled steps backwards. "I told you I'm not working anymore tonight."

"Hush," Elam whispered taking his finger to his lip.

"What are you doing down here anyway? I thought Hank stayed back here in the storeroom."

"He does," she answered motioning toward him lying in bed. "But I come down here when I've had a long night so nobody knows where to find me. By the way, how did you know where I was?"

"I didn't," Elam answered. "I was looking for Hank. But since you're already awake I'll talk to you. What rooms are those two new men that Laughlin hired staying in, Bear and Perkins?"

"Bear is in room five, and Perkins was in eight when I left him last night."

"Who they got standing guard?"

"Smitty's up in the bell-tower over at the church."

Elam nodded. "That's why he wasn't at the livery." Turning back to the door, he waved for Luke and Cork to come in and when they had, the three men crossed to the door leading into the saloon. But before entering, Elam turned to Luke, "Bear's in five." Then looking at Cork, he whispered, "You take Perkins; he's in room eight." The door opened with a loud squeak. They walked through placing one foot down easy in front of the other, then at right angle, they turned and eased along behind the bar to the end and crossed to the foot of the stairs. Taking one step at a time they started their climb careful not to make a sound. At the top Elam drew up in front of Maxwell Laughlin's room which was directly across the hall from room five where Luke stopped. Cork eased on down the dark hall to room four. Dropping to the floor with his back against that wall, he pointed his shotgun straight at the door across the hall leading into room eight. With everyone in place, they waited, giving the sun time to rise in hopes of having a little more light to work with. But after hearing a stir in Laughlin's room, Elam knew it was time to start the show. He took a deep, ragged breath and let it out slow. Then raising a foot, he let it fly and it made contact with the door, forcing it open with a loud bang, the force ripping it from its hinges. Stepping into the doorway, Elam pulled the trigger at a shadow rising from the bed, and it instantly fell back in place. Down the hall the door to room eight flung open, and Cork let go with both barrels of his shotgun sending whoever it was standing there flying backwards though the air. And in front of room five, Luke waited but the door never opened and there was no sound. Moments passed, then standing off to one side, Luke slowly reached down and worked the knob and gave the door a push. Slowly and with great caution, he stuck his head around the door frame and peeked in to find the room was empty. "There's nobody in here," he called out. Quickly they checked the rest of the room to find all of them empty too. Getting back to Maxwell Laughlin's room, Elam entered and crossed to the bed; he threw the covers back to find not Laughlin as he had expected but a man he'd never seen before—a tall slender man with long red hair.

The end of the gunplay soon brought Flo up the stairs in nothing more that her night clothes to see how it had turned out. She identified the man in Laughlin's room as Max Bear and the other dead man as Sam Perkins. The two gunfighters were both dead, but Maxwell Laughlin was nowhere to be found. "Maybe he drug out during the night," Elam suggested. Then after giving it some thought, he looked at Flo and asked, "Where's Hank. Why didn't he come up with you?" Then it hit him; he had not got a good look at the man she had said was Hank. "Was that Laughlin?" he asked. Reaching, he grabbed her by the arm and yanked her toward him. "Flo, if it was, you better tell me now."

She nodded her head. "I wanted to tell you, honest, Elam, but he said if I did he would kill me."

"Where's he at now? Where did he go?"

"He's gone to the livery. He's on his way to Caster."

"Luke," Elam called out. "Let's go, your man's trying to get away; if he ain't already gone, you'll find 'im down at the livery."

Luke broke down the stairs in a dead run with Elam and Cork right behind him. He jerked the doors open and ran out onto the boardwalk, just in time to see Maxwell Laughlin ride from the livery. "Look, there he is, but he's gettin' away," he yelled.

"Maybe not," Elam roared, pushing Luke aside, he drew his Winchester up, letting it come to rest alongside the support pole to steady it. He took aim and pulled the trigger. The horse staggered then flipped going head over heels. Maxwell Laughlin hit the ground hard and, after coming to a sliding stop, scrambled to his feet. But knowing it was all over, he stood waiting as Luke walked down the middle of the street toward him. With only twenty feet between them, Luke stopped with his feet spread wide his hand already fixed over the butt of his six-gun. "Laughlin," Luke called out. "Fill your hand."

"Now hold on, Luke," Laughlin said. "I don't know what you're talking about. I ain't got no fight with you. That deal between me and your paw was a good deal. And I swear to you I don't know who killed 'im. I have an idea though; I think it was Barton or Quint McKuen. I don't know that for a fact, but I can tell you for sure it wasn't me."

"Oh, they did it all right, but you told 'em to. And now

I'm going to kill you whether you draw your gun or not. So go ahead and reach for it; the least you can do is die like a man."

"You're asking for trouble, boy," Laughlin yelled. "I'm faster than you—you ain't got a chance."

"That might be, Laughlin, but you'll never know until you try."

By now several people had gathered around. Laughlin looked into the crowd. "Ain't somebody going to stop him—somebody shoot him; he's wanted for murder. Hell, this is Luke Ludd; he killed three men in cold blood right down the street there."

"No, he didn't, Laughlin," Leroy Radford spoke up from the back of the crowd. "And you know he didn't, and I've already had the charges dropped."

"Why, you cowardly little snake—" Laughlin said and in the same breath, he dropped his hand for his gun. But he was way too slow. Before he even touched the butt, a bullet had already ripped through his chest tearing at his heart and lungs, and another had struck him in the belly. He was still standing, but dead. He tried to speak but only blood came from his mouth; then his knees gave way and he crumbled to the ground. Luke holstered his still smoking six-gun and walked from the dusty street of the little town of Rising Star in the direction of the bridge and the cotton-wood where he had left Mousy. They mounted and started the long ride home. As they rode to within sight, Loraine came running from the barn. "I need to use your horse for a little while," Luke said as Cork stepped from the saddle, then looking at Loraine, he said, "Well, if we're going to take that ride, you better come on."

She smiled, and, with her paw giving her a hand, she pulled up into the saddle. They rode off side by side in the direction of the creek and all of those big beautiful pecan trees where they had spent many a day together. But the thought of the way this ride would end forced the smile from Loraine's face, for she knew that when it was over Luke would be gone. "Luke, now that you've got your paw's place back, what are you going to do with it," she asked. "Sell it?"

"No, I would never sell it, but I have been thinking about maybe giving it to you."

Her mouth fell open with surprise. "To me?" she asked. "Lord, I don't know what I'd do with it. I can't work it without help, and Paw's got his hands full looking after our place. If I knew that Uncle Elam was going to stay I might get him to help me, but you know him—here today, gone tomorrow."

"Well, I might just have an answer to all of that Loraine. How would you feel if I stayed around and gave you a hand? What would you think about something like that. Hell, if you want to and will have me, we might even get married." Luke drew up and stepped from his horse. Walking around he helped Loraine down. Taking her in his arms, he said, "With all my heart I love you, Loraine Langtry, and I'd be honored if you'd be my wife."

Hearing his words, she kicked him playfully on the leg and said, "Luke Ludd, I don't ever want to see you again." Laughing, she fell into his arms and said, "I love you, Luke, and yes, for ever and a day, I'll be your wife."